Heritage Woods
Library
withdrawn

nwonbrtiw

THE SECRET SHACK

To - Heritagewoods

ELLENOR SHEPHERD

Ellenor Shepherd 2014

WestBow Press
A DIVISION OF THOMAS NELSON
& ZONDERVAN

Copyright © 2016 Ellenor Eubanks Shepherd.

All rights reserved. No part of this book may be used or reproduced by any means, graphic, electronic, or mechanical, including photocopying, recording, taping or by any information storage retrieval system without the written permission of the author except in the case of brief quotations embodied in critical articles and reviews.

Scripture taken from the King James Version of the Bible.

WestBow Press books may be ordered through booksellers or by contacting:

WestBow Press
A Division of Thomas Nelson & Zondervan
1663 Liberty Drive
Bloomington, IN 47403
www.westbowpress.com
1 (866) 928-1240

Because of the dynamic nature of the Internet, any web addresses or links contained in this book may have changed since publication and may no longer be valid. The views expressed in this work are solely those of the author and do not necessarily reflect the views of the publisher, and the publisher hereby disclaims any responsibility for them.

Any people depicted in stock imagery provided by Thinkstock are models, and such images are being used for illustrative purposes only. Certain stock imagery © Thinkstock.

ISBN: 978-1-5127-2932-0 (sc)
ISBN: 978-1-5127-2933-7 (hc)
ISBN: 978-1-5127-2931-3 (e)

Library of Congress Control Number: 2016901702

Print information available on the last page.

WestBow Press rev. date: 02/22/2016

To my wonderful family:
My three sons, Clif, John, and Wes
My daughter-in-law, Molly
My grandsons, Harrison, Clay, and Peter
My granddaughters, Grace and Amelie

I have learned, in whatsoever state I am, therewith to be content.

—Philippians 4:11 (KJV)

Your present situation may not be to your liking. If God wants you elsewhere, He will lead you there, providing you are amenable to His will. But if He wants you where you are, He will help you adjust. He will make you content, even grateful for present opportunities. Learn the great art of doing the best you can. In this way, you learn how to reach the better condition, or how to make your present condition better.

—*Life Lifters*, Jonathan T. Olakunle

Who Am I?

Who am I?
Where am I going?
Who cares
if I get there?

Who will know?
He will know.

I am His child.
I walk with Him.
He watches my journey.
He welcomes me there.

He offers His hand.
He gives His love.
There are no restraints.
He asks nothing of me.

How can I repay
this gift of His life,
freely given,
no strings attached?

His overwhelming love
for my unworthiness,
His pain, His suffering
beyond my understanding,

to make me free—

What can I say
in response to His gift?

Live as He lived,
my life for His,
love as He loved,
give as He gave.

Who am I?
Where am I going?
Who knows
if I get there?

He will know …
and care

—Ellenor E. Shepherd

ACKNOWLEDGMENTS

I am deeply indebted to my son, Dr. Clif Flynn, who fine-tuned my words, patiently corrected my grammar, pushed me for clarity, and insisted on more when I was satisfied with less. Thank you for your support and encouragement during the writing of my first novel.

Special thanks to my dear friend, Barbara Heilig, who is always willing to read my story, make corrections, and offer honest feedback to keep me on the right track.

And to Spencer Bridges, who put my manuscript into acceptable form, I am so grateful.

PROLOGUE

He stood by the seashore staring at the raging water without seeing. Tears rushed down his cheeks, but no sound escaped his lips. He was only twelve years old, but the pain and loss resonated far beyond his young years. What he felt at this moment would follow him the rest of his life. No child should ever be burdened with such a heavy load, nor should children bear their burdens alone—he had no one to answer his questions, no one with whom to share his feelings, and no one to embrace him with a warm, loving hug.

The tide was beginning to come in, sending waves of water swirling around his skinny legs. Finally, a huge wave crested and crashed at his knees, knocking him off balance and back into the real world.

Slowly, he backed out of the water, turned, and walked across the hills of sand, returning to the small, empty shack tucked away in the dense vegetation. Just before entering, he heard a whimpering sound nearby. It became louder, drawing him into the thicket...

CHAPTER 1

Where had the years gone? He felt the pain of the twelve-year-old. He felt the fear and the aloneness once again. He longed for the warmth and comforting hugs that briefly took away his pain.

When he and his parents had visited the seashore each summer, they had stayed in his grandparents' twenty-two room, gray-shingled cottage, the largest dwelling in the town of Goose. Covering almost a city block with its rambling style and beautifully landscaped gardens, it was often mistaken for a local hotel. David, however, spent his days exploring the Outer Banks until, at age twelve, he discovered the small dilapidated structure hidden away in the jungle-like vegetation toward the east end of the island. From that moment on, David Livingstone Ward, only child of a well-known catalog magnate, took on a different personality—and even a different name. He became Daniel. And he claimed the shack as his own.

His parents never questioned where he was all day nor what he had been doing. They were much too busy protecting their role as the leaders of the seaside social circuit. Mrs. Harriet Ward was constantly entertaining and planning events in order to maintain her social status. Most of the other ladies, who were summer residents also, found little to like about Harriet. They considered her arrogant and controlling, which made her company even more intolerable. And they talked about her behind her back, genuinely concerned that she never had any idea where her son was during the day. They often wondered how David Sr. could tolerate anyone as obnoxious as Harriet, especially when she had too much to drink, which was often. "He must be a good and patient man," someone in the group always offered.

Little by little, David began to sneak to the shack a sheet, a towel, some food, and other essentials until he had stocked this almost-fallen-down, sparsely furnished shack rather nicely. The two tiny rooms could boast only a rusty iron, a sagging bed, a worn upholstered chair, a rough table with four mismatched chairs, and a temperamental old stove. The old, oval, braided rug had raveled beyond repair, and the curtains at the small windows were faded and tattered. To Daniel, however, it became a refuge where he often wondered what it would be like to have parents who cared about him. He yearned to have parents who would say those longed-for words, "I love you," and who would occasionally give him one of those big bear hugs his friends got from their parents. Daniel took his notebook and pen to the shack and spent hours writing stories. His English teacher had encouraged him to write, but his parents never asked to see or read any of his compositions. Life was good for Daniel; being alone was not a negative for him. One midsummer day, Daniel was walking along the water's edge when he heard a soft, whimpering sound. At first he ignored it, but it soon grew louder and louder, drawing him in its direction toward a covert of trees in the thick vegetation, where he discovered a girl who looked to be about his age. Huddled down in a hole carved out in the sand, she was dressed in faded shorts and a shirt two sizes too small, but the distress in her voice captured his attention and concern. She was startled when he spoke, and she started to run away. But something about Daniel's voice seemed to make her feel safe and unafraid. He learned that her name was Laney and that her mother, Mona, was a waitress at the popular seafood restaurant on the island. The owner allowed them to live upstairs over the restaurant. Daniel asked Laney why she was crying, and she promptly responded, "I'm not allowed to tell. In fact, no one knows that one night I overheard a conversation my mother was having with a strange man. She became very angry with me when I asked her about it, and she said, 'If you tell anyone about it, we might be killed.'" Daniel immediately felt a connection with this soft-spoken and fragile young girl, and he was touched that she trusted him with her secret.

"Laney, my name is Daniel. Come and let me show you my very own little secret house. I have never invited anyone to visit me before today."

Laney followed Daniel as he led the way through the thick vegetation until the shack came into view. Daniel held the door properly as he motioned for Laney to enter. Not used to anything fine or of value, Laney complimented him on his beautiful cottage. Daniel was touched by the sincerity in her voice.

"What do you do here all day?" asked Laney. "Don't you get lonely?"

"Never," said Daniel. "I often write stories for hours."

"Will you read some of your stories to me?" Laney timidly asked, as if afraid he might ridicule her or refuse.

Ecstatic, but in utter disbelief, Daniel blurted out, "You mean you honestly would like to hear some of my writings?"

"Of course," she answered in her quiet manner. "I've never had anyone read to me."

And this became a daily practice. Laney would come to the shack, often bringing some food from the restaurant for each of them. After they had eaten, she would curl up in the old chair by the window, smiling contentedly as Daniel read, often imagining she lived in this shack.

One day they decided to take a break to go swimming while the ocean was calm. They began playing in the surf like most typical twelve-year-olds, diving under the water and surprising the other, or they would take turns diving from each other's shoulders. You could hear their cries of joy and delight up and down the beach. They were beginning to get hungry, but Daniel went under one more time. When he surfaced, he came up right in front of Laney—and much closer than he had intended. He had had so much fun that impulsively he gave Laney a huge bear hug, which seemed to Daniel to be the most natural thing in the whole world to do. Laney, however, was shocked and just stood still, not saying anything. Twelve-year-old Daniel felt stirrings in his heart that he had never experienced before. To cover his surprise, he grabbed Laney's hand and said, "Let's go eat."

The rest of that day, they were a little subdued and shy with each other, but the next day their relationship returned to normal. The days passed all too quickly, and it was soon time for Daniel's parents to close the summerhouse and go back home.

Daniel told Laney, "This is the best summer I have ever had, and I will miss you and the good times we've had together." Laney began to cry. Daniel put his arms around her and said, "Don't cry, Laney. The months will pass quickly, and we'll soon be back enjoying each other again." Laney put her head on Daniel's shoulder, and they just sat quietly for a while until, to his own surprise, Daniel leaned over to give Laney a sweet kiss right on the lips. They got up, and Laney hugged Daniel. She then turned, walked slowly out of the shack, and never looked back.

Daniel had often wondered who had owned this deserted little shack. No one had come near it the entire summer. He made a vow that somehow he would find a way to own the shack someday. As Daniel was gathering up all his belongings, he smiled broadly, remembering how much he liked kissing Laney.

Daniel was disappointed and quite sad when his parents informed him they would not be coming back to the Outer Banks the next summer. Later he learned his parents were planning to sell his grandparents' charming old cottage where he had stayed each summer as long as he could remember. His mother wanted a home in the Dominican Republic to have a more prestigious address, which meant he would be spending the winters in a boarding school and summers in a well-known camp. Daniel was devastated. The two things that meant the most to him were now going to be snatched away—Laney, the only person in the entire world who understood him, and his own private space where he could write without hearing his mother and father argue. His parents, especially his mother, would be appalled if they had any idea that their son, David Livingstone Ward, found happiness in a rundown, barely furnished old shack hidden in the dense island vegetation. What David did not know was that they had gotten a background check on Laney, and had found out she was a poor girl who lived above a restaurant and that her mother was a lowly, divorced waitress. They were in disbelief that their son, who had been raised having the best of everything, including friends at the top of the social register, found any pleasure in this relationship. Harriet, David's mother, usually faced her parenting problems or any other unpleasant issues fortified with a cocktail, proudly declaring that she did not use tranquilizers, as did many of her friends.

Daniel wrote Laney immediately, explaining what had happened and how much he would miss her and their time together. Daniel was eager to hear from Laney, but the weeks dragged on and no letter came. Months passed, and it became obvious that he probably was not going to hear from her. He actually felt like he was missing a part of himself.

Laney wondered why she had not heard from Daniel. She had believed him when he said he would write. She had trusted him to do what he had promised, so it hurt even more deeply when the anticipated letter never came. This new aloneness was unlike any she had ever known.

Laney

Laney had never known her father, since the man who had impregnated her mother disappeared as soon as he learned she was expecting. Laney had been a good baby, as if she knew there was only a mother to care for her. Her mother, Mona, worked on the island as a waitress and was allowed to bring Laney to work. Laney was an adorable, loveable child and all the waitresses and cooks claimed her as their own. At the early age of four, she began asking how to cook certain foods but no one took her seriously. However, Laney's determined nature kicked in, and when she begged relentlessly for two days, they realized she was quite serious. Whenever one of the cooks had a little free time, he or she would show Laney how to prepare a certain dish. She was a natural in the kitchen, but her favorite time was when she was baking. By the time she was ten, Laney often prepared muffins or the fixings for a pie or other delectable baked goods. She loved going to the restaurant as soon as school was out, and she couldn't wait each year for summer to come so she could spend the day cooking or learning

David

David had learned at an early age that his mother was not the nurturing type; in fact, she barely acknowledged he existed. If her friends came over, David was relegated to his room until the social event had ended and all of the guests had departed. Harriet forbade David to come into the bedroom where she and David's father slept. A local woman was hired to come in at eight in the morning to prepare breakfast so Harriet wasn't disturbed. Occasionally, David Sr. came into the kitchen where David preferred to eat and tried to talk with him, but he was away so much of the time on business that he was almost a stranger to David. David usually replied to his questions with the appropriate "No, sir," or "Yes, sir." David felt the lack of spontaneity, knowing the attempt to converse was forced, but he simply accepted the situation the way it was.

Harriet stayed up late at night enjoying her cocktails, and then slept until noon. David liked to get up early and eat a big breakfast before taking off for the day. He routinely packed his favorite knapsack, the not-so-fancy soiled one, always with a pen and a pad, a sandwich for lunch, and a snack for later. Inevitably, he wore a swimsuit under his shorts since he opted for an impromptu swim now and then. Off he went each day, knowing no one cared where he was going and no one cared if or when he might return. Fortunately, David spent the majority of his time writing, or observing and thinking about what to write.

Laney

Soon after Daniel left, Laney questioned her mother again about what she had overheard, and Mona exploded with anger. In her somewhat inebriated condition, she yelled menacing threats at Laney, causing her to be overcome with hurt and fear. Laney was devastated and had no idea what made her mother react so uncontrollably. These outbursts were becoming more frequent and each one more violent. Laney knew that the dark side of her mother was brought on by drinking too much, and her drinking was escalating. This last scene convinced Laney it was no longer safe to be in her mother's presence. Quickly she tossed a few necessary items in her shabby old suitcase. She quietly slipped out and went to the only place where she was unafraid—the secret shack. Her mother disappeared the same night.

When Laney delivered her muffins two days later, Mr. Mac told her told her that her mother had vanished during the night without leaving a forwarding address or an explanation. Mr. Mac felt a deep sorrow and concern for this dear girl who was alone at such a tender young age.

Laney managed to hold back the tears until she ran inside the shack and closed the door, then she cried out, "Dear God, what have

I done to deserve this?" She began to wonder if she had, in some way, provoked this frightening and hurtful situation. However, after much reflection and introspection, and with wisdom that defied her age, Laney concluded she was a victim of circumstances beyond her control. But the hurt for her mother lingered. Her positive outlook simply did not allow her to succumb to gloom. Instead, she turned to cleaning and fixing up the shack to make it livable. She crawled into bed that night tired and sad, but not defeated. Before falling to sleep, she prayed, "Thank you, Lord for giving me a place to live and please take care of my mother wherever she may be … and Daniel. Amen." Laney tried hard to control her tears, but a few escaped and rolled slowly down her cheeks before she finally closed her eyes and fell into a long-overdue sleep.

CHAPTER 2

Five years later, David's father (most likely to salve his own guilt) gave his son a bright red BMW convertible for a graduation gift. When summer arrived, David and two of his friends, Mike and Craig, decided to drive down to the Outer Banks for a few days. After driving an hour, David stopped at a used car lot on the outskirts of a small country town and got out to look at the cars. He quickly chose a 1989 faded blue Chevy, gave the owner a deposit, and asked if he could leave his car there for several days. David was appreciative of his graduation gift, but he preferred a less showy, inexpensive car. He never wanted to be referred to as "that spoiled rich kid." He used a fictitious name and address for the deposit slip, which he placed in the glove compartment of the convertible along with his wallet. For a few days, he was going to be Daniel White from Norfolk, Virginia. Mike and Craig's parents were always at the club or on a trip, so the boys were free to do whatever they wanted. David's parents were out of the country, so he didn't have to report to anyone. His memory of Laney had faded through the years, but as he approached the beach, he suddenly envisioned that sweet fragile young girl who had been such a huge part of his life five years ago. That night he suggested to his buddies that the Sea Wind Restaurant was a great place to eat seafood. Secretly he was hoping Laney might be there. Disappointed that he had not seen Laney, he decided to ask the long-time cashier if she would give Laney a message. The cashier laughed and said, "Sonny, her mom left here three summers ago under strange circumstances, and we have not seen or heard from her since. We do know Laney lives in a secret place by herself, but we rarely see her, except when she delivers her delicious baked goods." David thanked the cashier, and he and his friends went back to the motel. The next morning David got up at six o'clock and quietly slipped out. He quickly found his way to the special little shack he had loved and adopted as his own that last summer. He noticed a flower box on the front window overflowing with color. The door was painted a very bright but cheerful blue. It was obvious someone was living in the shack. Feeling a bit shy, he knocked on the door, and when it opened, he was at a loss for words.

A lovely young woman stood there, but when she said, "May I help you?" in that unforgettable soft voice, David grinned from ear to ear.

He blurted, "You're Laney, and you are even more gorgeous than I remembered. Why didn't you answer my letter?"

"Daniel, is it really you? I can't believe you're actually here! A letter—what letter?" Her words rushed out, tumbling over each other in her astonishment. "Oh no, I'm sure I know what happened. I should have figured that out sooner. After you and I had been together every day for two months, your dad came by and offered my mom a thousand dollars if she would keep us from seeing each other. She was thrilled; she took it, all right, but she didn't try to stop me from seeing you. When I found out, I was angry, disappointed, and hurt. We had an argument about—well, about something else. She scared me, and ... I came here to live. I hope you don't mind."

"No, the house is not mine yet, but I have saved money for years so I have enough to buy it now."

Laney looked crestfallen. "I'm very happy for you. I know that's what you always wanted. I'll try to move out as quickly as possible. May I have a couple of days to find someplace else to live?"

"Laney, I would never ask you to leave as long as I can come now and then."

"Thank you, Daniel. You are still so kind. I promise to take the best care of your house." Laney knew she was too emotional to say anything else without crying.

"I guess I should tell you now that my real name is David, not Daniel. May I come back tonight and visit with you for a while? I'll tell you the whole story."

"I would like that very much, David."

David left reluctantly, counting the hours till he could return, never realizing that his life would change drastically later that day. He, Mike, and Craig decided to drive to the other end of the island to see the wild horses. As they rounded a curve, singing at the top of their voices, a big white power company truck came into view, straddling the center line. David blew his horn, but to no avail. In a matter of seconds, the power truck rammed head on into David's car. The old Chevy spun out of control before crashing into a light pole. A terrible silence followed. No one in the car moved. The driver of the utility truck came to, called 911, and got out to check the passengers in the car he had hit. He knew he was at fault and most likely would be sentenced to a significant time in prison once they saw his previous record. Fabricating a different story, relieving himself of any responsibility, was effortless, since no one in the crash could counter his version. Scanning the inside of the car to see if there was anything worth taking, he grabbed the young men's wallets and glove compartment contents and stuffed it all into his pockets, congratulating himself on obtaining new identity information so easily. When he heard the sirens approach, he quickly jumped back into the truck, pretending to be in pain.

It was not a pretty picture—the front seat passenger, Craig, was missing; Mike, the passenger in the back seat, was in a strange, unnatural position and not moving. Not only was David's body pinned under the steering wheel but his legs were trapped by the car engine, which had crunched under the impact. His pulse was faint, and the EMTs worked ceaselessly to keep him alive while they tried to get him out of the wrecked car. It took two hours for the paramedics to cut David free, but he was released at last and quickly transferred to the helicopter that flew him directly to Duke Hospital on the mainland, where a trauma team was standing by. Lucky for him, he was unconscious the whole time.

Eventually, Craig's body was recovered from the shallow canal that ran parallel to the coastal road. There was no sign of life. Mike had apparently died instantly upon impact. David was barely alive when he arrived at the huge medical complex. The doctors worked way into the night to stabilize the young man. Since his license apparently had been stolen, parents or next of kin were oblivious to what happened to David and the hospital had no way of identifying him.

Laney, though, had heard the sirens, but dismissed the sound, thinking sadly that another carload of teenagers with too much to drink had lost control on the curve.

She was excited about spending time with Daniel. She had baked an apple pie and cleaned the already spotless shack until she was exhausted. When Daniel was an hour late, Laney began searching for reasons to explain why he had not come or called. She was certain he had found her unattractive, especially, since he was so handsome and most likely quite used to being pursued by many gorgeous girls. Midnight came, and Laney finally gave up and went to bed. Sleep eluded her that night, and as she watched the sunrise the next morning, she was sure David would not return. That innocent little twelve-year-old girl had waited for years to see Daniel. Now that he had not honored the date, she accepted the reality that, as an adult, he would never find meaning in their relationship other than a summer of childhood fun.

CHAPTER 3

Laney had developed quite a reputation for her delectable pies and other baked goods, and soon people began to hire her to bake for special occasions. After graduating from high school, she continued working as a waitress at the Sea Wind Restaurant at night and enrolled in the county technical college culinary program during the day. Two years later, she surpassed all of her instructors, and they graciously agreed she had met all of their expectations with her cooking skills. Laney saved every penny she made, with the exception of what she needed for food and a limited wardrobe, usually purchased at the local Bargain Box.

Realizing her penchant for baking, the restaurant hired her to cook all of their baked delicacies. Often she worked late into the night after she had gotten off work. Laney had become even more beautiful with maturity, and nearly every single man on the island—and those visiting—tried unsuccessfully to date her. No one could fathom why she preferred being alone. Laney had always felt safe on the island, but she became uneasy after she rode her bike home early one evening and found an open window. She did a most unusual thing, contrary to her independent nature—she confided in Mr. Macadoo, who was the only person she trusted. Mr. Mac worried about Laney living alone in such an isolated place and offered her the apartment over the restaurant, but she politely declined. After a couple of weeks had passed, she began to relax, until one night upon returning home, she saw a figure darting out from the back of the shack and running into the dense vegetation. Laney checked and found everything was intact, but she wondered who this person was and what he wanted. She had nothing of any value, and it never occurred to her to fear that she could be the target.

CHAPTER 4

The young unidentified man, a patient at Duke Hospital, was dubbed Mr. X. He vacillated between life and death for two weeks before, to the amazement of the doctors, he began to show a slight improvement. No one had come to see him or called to inquire about his condition. He had no identification when he arrived at the hospital and none was found in the mangled car. The cops suspected someone had come upon the scene believing that everyone was dead and took advantage of the opportunity by stealing the identities of the three young men. David's wreck had occurred two months before he was to enter Harvard, the college of his parent's choice. Since David was an unidentified person with no recollection of who he was or that he was to attend Harvard, of course the college was still expecting him. One week after the designated freshman registration time had passed without David registering, a routine official letter was sent to his parents asking if he had decided not to attend. If so, the school requested a letter to that effect so another freshman might have the privilege of entering. Mr. Ward was concerned, but Mrs. Ward was too busy maintaining her social status on the island to give it any serious thought. Mr. Ward, however, tried to find David, but with no success. He realized that when they had left the Outer

Banks, David was quite upset and sad, but when he had tried to talk with his son about his feelings, David always politely said he did not want to discuss it. Mr. Ward hired private investigators and called in the FBI, but not a hint of David's whereabouts was detected. Mr. Ward lived every day with the anguish and the fear that his son might not be alive. He prayed fervently for forgiveness and for knowledge that he and David could be reconciled. David would have been surprised to learn his father knew how to pray. Their family had never attended church, with the exception of putting in an appearance at the Christmas service. It was only after David had met Abraham, his therapist, that he was introduced to the power of prayer.

David Livingstone Ward, Sr., had inherited the nationally known catalog company founded by his father. He was a handsome man, pursued by the opposite sex almost to the point of embarrassment. Soon after he graduated from college and began working in his father's business, a young woman employed there had her eye on David. She was a beautiful young woman who knew how to get her way with the opposite sex. As soon as she saw David and learned who he was, she knew he would be her next conquest. What a catch he would be! Just think, she would be Mrs. David Livingstone Ward, as high up on the social register as possible. Harriet had always tried to associate with those who were well educated, wealthy, and lived on a higher plane. Since she was so attractive, she never lacked for dates with men at the top of the social list. A fast learner, Harriet observed and mimicked the people she hung out with until no one ever thought to question her pedigree. So, when David met Harriet, it did not take long for her to completely charm and control him. In six months, a huge wedding took place, much to the chagrin of the Wards, who had investigated this woman and found her background to be quite unacceptable. David Ward was essentially a good man who had fallen unknowingly for a conniving woman climbing the proverbial social ladder. When he realized he had been hoodwinked, the knot had already been tied and baby David, Jr. was on the way, so he decided to make the best of a terrible mistake. During their marriage, his biggest fault was giving in to Mrs. Ward in order to maintain peace and curtail her thirst for alcohol. He loved his son deeply and wanted to shield him from his mother's weakness, but there was a chasm between father and son that made communication impossible.

In the third week, David roused briefly, spoke one word, "Laney," and drifted back into no-man's land. More and more often, he opened his eyes and uttered another word—"Where?" The attending nurse explained to him that he had been in a wreck and now was in Duke Hospital. That seemed to satisfy him, and he would return to the darkness. David was unaware that he had lost a leg or that the doctors were able to save the other leg, although it was badly injured. It would need an undetermined number of surgeries with no assurance of success. And, until he was fully conscious, there was the question of how much damage the injury had inflicted on the brain.

CHAPTER 5

Laney had long forgotten what she had heard that night many years ago when her mother found out she had been listening and became very angry and threatened Laney. But tonight, while riding her bike home, for some unknown reason, she began remembering it vividly until she was startled suddenly by a noise, bringing her quickly back to the present. Laney spotted a man dressed in what appeared to be a Beach Patrol uniform, sneaking away from the rear of the shack. After she managed to unlock the door, jump inside to the safety of the shack, and relock the door, she was shaking, and for the first time in years, she didn't know what to do. Should she call the Beach Patrol or Mr. Mac, or should she keep quiet and hope it was just a beach bum looking for food? Opting for the latter, she checked every square inch of the shack and, satisfied that he had not been inside, got ready for bed. She was exhausted but unable to sleep, so finally, she got up and started baking, which was her calming tool. While mixing the ingredients for the scones the way her mother had taught her, another forgotten memory flashed through her mind. As she placed the scones in the oven, all of a sudden she saw her mother doing the same thing while talking to a certain man who lived there on the island. The flashback was what she had overheard as a child, the incident that had caused her mother to threaten her. That was the reason she had run down the road and hidden in the dense vegetation until Daniel found her. She spoke aloud, "I won't go there. I refuse to allow myself to think about Daniel." But she wondered if the man who had been involved with her mother was the same man who was nosing around her home tonight. Perhaps he thought she might have something that would prove what she had overheard that awful night. Or maybe he was simply trying to hurt her or frighten her so she would leave the area? *What am I to do?* thought Laney. "Maybe it won't happen again," she repeated out loud, trying to convince herself. Laney sat down at the kitchen table to wait for the scones to bake.

The smell of smoke woke her up and, of course, the scones were charred beyond recognition.

CHAPTER 6

The next day, the man the nurses called Mr. X was so agitated that he had to be restrained. Near the end of the day, he began to calm down and tried to speak. Soon he was putting words together to make simple sentences. "My name?" he would ask, but sadly, no one knew. Social Services had contacted authorities on the Outer Banks, but no one there remembered him. They did remember that the couple with the biggest home there had had one child, but no one knew where they lived since they had divorced and gone their separate ways. As Mr. X slipped in and out of his sleepy state, now and then he would utter, "Laney." The nurse and staff wondered if this Laney were a friend, a girlfriend, a relative, or who. They had adopted this young man who obviously had no one who cared about him or gave him extra attention. The nurses would sit with him on their breaks and read to him, hoping to trigger a thought or memory. Little did they know that Mr. X was an aspiring writer who had planned to major in English in college. They were dreading the day when he would be alert and stable enough physically and emotionally to be told he had lost a leg.

One week later, Mr. X was talking and making sense, but he still could not remember his name. The doctor explained that he was suffering from amnesia and that his memory would come back, but he could not predict when. "But, son," said Dr. Warner, "there is something else you do not know about that happened to you in the accident. To be truthful, there is no easy way to tell you. To put it bluntly, you have lost your left leg."

Mr. X did not respond. He just stared. He did not blink. Finally, after what seemed like an eternity, he muttered, "What about my other leg?"

"It was badly injured and will require several surgeries and much rehab, and then it still may not work well. Only time and your attitude will determine the extent of your recovery."

"You know you just knocked me for a loop, Doc? Can I have a pen and a pad? I need to write about this."

"Certainly. Nurse, would you please get our patient a pen and a pad?"

"Thanks, Doc." Mr. X turned his head toward the wall and did not speak again that day, even when the nurse brought him a pen and pad as requested.

Mr. X remained in the same position for the rest of the day with pen and pad in his hand, staring at the wall but not seeing. He did not move, nor speak, nor eat, nor answer any questions, as if he were in a catatonic state. The news of losing his leg was too much to bear alone, and there was no one who cared. *Laney cares,* flashed through his mind and he turned his head and connected with the world again. "Why did I say that? Who is Laney? She must be someone special with a caring heart." Mr. X picked up his pad and wrote one word that night—Laney. The next day he wrote, "No leg, my leg is gone." Then he asked on paper, "What do they do with legs that are no longer connected? Do they have a funeral service for the leg? It was once a living thing. Is it tossed into the garbage? Is it given to the animals as a special treat?" All kinds of bizarre thoughts raced across Mr. X's troubled and agonized mind. And then, from out of nowhere—or so it seemed—came the words, "Thank you, Lord, for my other leg, badly mangled as it may be. Thank you."

CHAPTER 7

Laney kept thinking about the silhouette of the man who had been hanging around her home. She was sure she had seen someone his shape and size before, but she had yet to match a name or face with it. Then she remembered thinking she had been followed by one of the Beach Patrol officers, but she soon discounted that idea.

Today was the day she was to meet with Mr. Mac to ask if she could rent the small building he owned next door. Laney had dreamed of opening a bakery for years. She needed just the right name. So far, nothing had resonated with her.

On the way home after work, Laney noticed a Beach Patrol cop following her again. He kept his distance, but his intentions were obvious. This time Laney noticed that his uniform and bike were not exactly like the others, and she felt a sudden urge to get home ASAP to secure the shack. Could this man possibly be connected to her mother in some way? Laney quickly entered the shack and locked up the best she could. Peering out of each window, she saw no sign of anyone. Laney feared she was becoming paranoid. Maybe sharing these concerns and fears with Mr. Mac would help put all the coincidences into perspective.

Mr. Mac was thrilled when Laney presented her pitch. "Laney, you are just like a daughter to me, and I am so proud of you. You know I will do anything to help you with whatever you need."

"Oh, Mr. Mac, no one has ever offered to help me. That means everything!" She gave him a huge hug.

Thoughts of naming the bakery and worrying about the long list of things to be addressed before she could consider opening were replaced soon by a deep sleep. Laney awoke with a start in the wee hours of the next morning talking to herself. "The Sweet Shack—The Sweet Shack. Perfect," she murmured, closing her eyes and drifting back to sleep. Dreams bombarded her sleep, dreams of a twelve-year-old boy and a twelve-year-old girl who had connected at once because each needed someone. Just before parting, a sweet unexpected kiss from Daniel left a lasting effect on Laney, preventing her from ever having the desire to date other men. Only Laney knew the reason why.

Laney couldn't wait to begin fixing up The Sweet Shack. She had more ideas than she had money, but she had been gathering appropriate objects for two years, scavenging yard sales, items along the roadside, attending church rummage sales, and going anywhere there was an opportunity to get something for as little as possible. Her biggest expense would be an oven and stove, and that was cause for concern. Laney donned her painting clothes, grabbed the paint and paint brush, and headed for the Sweet Shack. Since she was in a coastal town, she opted for light and bright colors. The outside was to be a deep pink with white trim. Inside, seats, accented with black and white polka dotted fabric against white leather back cushions, gave it a happy look. A rustic sign with the name "The Sweet Shack" hung over the front door to welcome the hoped-for customers.

On the wall behind the counter, Laney hung an enlarged picture of the shack inscribed, "Daniel's Shack, 2001." Later when customers asked about the picture, Laney would smile sweetly and say simply, "It was a special place and time in my life," and then she would move on or change the subject. Recognizing the shack in the picture, Mr. Mac surmised Laney was using it, but he did not know Daniel was involved. He was confident, however, that when the time was right, Laney would confide in him.

Soon the bakery was ready to use except for one problem—it did not have a stove or an oven. Laney's savings were almost depleted. Mr. Mac knew her problem, and he and the entire community had come to respect and love this sweet young woman who had grown up alone, coping with life by herself. Mr. Mac asked Laney to come to work about two o'clock on Sunday to get ready for a special event. Upon arrival, he asked to see the inside of the Sweet Shack and Laney's latest addition. She loved to show off the Sweet Shack. While they were inside, someone knocked on the door, and when Laney opened it, Mr. Arnold from the appliance store and the entire community were gathered outside. In unison, they all yelled, "Special Delivery!" The stove and oven Laney had admired and coveted for so long were brought inside and connected. Laney was so touched and humbled by the generosity of these people and their gift that she was completely overcome with love for each one. She vowed at that moment to always give love where needed. She recalled a saying she had once read: "A gift is not a gift unless given away with love."

CHAPTER 8

Mr. X began communicating with the staff, but his darkest moments were when he was alone and wondering about his identity, his name, and if he had a family. The staff had started calling him Shakespeare, instead of Mr. X, since he wrote most of the time. They were thrilled that he did not have permanent brain damage.

A reporter at the *Durham Daily News*, looking for a story, had heard about this unidentified young man and his writings so he paid him a visit. "Hi! May I call you Shakespeare? I am Tom Willet, a news reporter, and I heard about your dilemma. I'd like to write a story about you. Maybe someone will recognize your picture and come forth with some pertinent information. What do you think?"

"Tom, to be honest, I'm almost afraid that someone who doesn't really know me will step up or someone claiming I've done something wrong ... I don't know ... It's scary."

"Well, Shakespeare, how about letting me read some of your writings that I'm hearing so much about? An analysis might help identify you."

"Okay, I'll let you read a couple of stories—one describing my feelings and one about the hospital."

"Thanks, buddy, that will do just fine. I'll just sit here and read them if you are more comfortable with that arrangement." Twenty minutes later, the man now known as Shakespeare looked over at Tom, who had not spoken once after beginning to read, and was astonished to see tears running down the cheeks of this veteran newspaperman. Tom was unabashed about his tears. He said, "Shakespeare, you have the gift. It has been a long time since I've felt such emotion and been so moved by the written word. Will you allow me to check with my editor to see if he will publish these? And Shakespeare, I would love to read more of your writings."

"Thank you, Tom. Feel free to take this notebook with you. Just please bring it back when you are finished."

Tom was eager to read all of Shakespeare's writings and spent his every free minute doing just that. Fascinated by the maturity of the writings, he shared them with his boss. Bob Curtis, editor of the *Durham Daily News*, was blown away by the young man's way with words, and he expressed his desire to meet him.

"If you don't think that Shakespeare would be upset, I would like to accompany you on your next visit."

"On the contrary, I am sure he would love to meet someone in your position who embraces what he loves most, writing."

The next day Shakespeare was to be fitted for a prosthesis, after which he would begin a limited workout in rehab. At least two more operations would be needed to, hopefully, restore sixty-five percent use of the remaining leg.

CHAPTER 9

Shakespeare did not want to go to therapy; he did not want to make a fool of himself; he did not want the world to see that he was missing a leg; he did not want ... But he was there, and he was introduced to his therapist, a young man named Abraham. Abraham spoke with an accent. He said, "I am happy to meet you, Shakespeare; I have heard your story and know you are a strong man."

Shakespeare did not want to engage in conversation; he simply wanted to get his therapy session over and return to his room. He grunted in response and looked the other way. Abraham was not offended. He had been one of the Lost Boys of Sudan, and his faith had faltered many times on the long, hot trek he had endured. Had it not been for one of the older boys reminding him of God's love, he too, would have given up. In his soft, kind voice, he announced, "Today, Shakespeare, we will talk about what you'll be doing the next few weeks and why. Then we will go through each exercise once or twice so you will know what to expect."

"Do what you have to do," mumbled Shakespeare.

Abraham explained as they moved along, and then he quietly said, "Thank you, Shakespeare, I am grateful to be your therapist. I will see you tomorrow at the same time. Go in peace."

Shakespeare wasn't sure what to think of this dark-skinned young therapist who spoke with an accent. He wondered where he called home. On the way back to his room, the nurse said, "You are very lucky to have Abraham as your therapist. He is one of the Lost Boys of Sudan, you know."

Shakespeare only said, "Oh?" He could not recall who they were. That night sleep would not come and he began to write silly poems ...

> I lost my leg
> I cannot walk
> But my mouth is big
> And I can still talk.

And then he scribbled:

> Oh leg, oh leg where did you go?
> I can't see you, but I feel my big toe.

This went on for a long time until suddenly he stopped, remembering the words a young girl once said to him: "We don't appreciate what we have until we lose it. But once we lose it, we need to thank God that we once had it." Who was this girl? Whose was she? Was his memory beginning to surface a little?

Shakespeare fell asleep near daybreak thinking about the words that this unknown girl in his life had shared. When he woke up, he felt somewhat connected to a place that had eluded him for many months. At first, Shakespeare went to therapy day after day reluctantly, but he actually began to grow fond of Abraham and looked forward to those torturous sessions. And torturous they were ... Shakespeare had never known such pain, but Abraham managed to talk him through the pain as he slowly led him in the direction of the Lord. Interrupting Abraham one day during therapy,

Shakespeare confessed, "I really know very little about the Lost Boys of Sudan; will you tell me all about your journey?"

And in his soft, melodic voice, Abraham began, all the while working with Shakespeare, sharing his unbelievably arduous and seemingly impossible trek across the desert. That day, no physical pain during therapy existed for Shakespeare, only the pain he felt deep inside for what Abraham had suffered. But Abraham never once alluded to his experience as painful; he always thanked God and credited Him for bringing him safely through that horrendous ordeal.

When Abraham had finished, Shakespeare, visibly touched, whispered, "Abraham, I didn't know. And all this time, you have listened to me patiently while I grumbled and complained and you never said a word. Tell me, who is this Lord or God you are always talking about?"

Abraham was the second person who had mentioned God to him. All Abraham would say the first few times Shakespeare raised the question was, "The God I know and love would never do anything hurtful or harmful to any of His children, and we are all God's children."

Shakespeare wrote it down on his pad and often pondered those words, until one day he had an epiphany. He exclaimed to an empty room, "I do have a father, I am God's child," and a great peace washed over him. The staff noticed a change in Shakespeare's attitude and demeanor. He seemed almost eager to go to rehab. The sessions were going quite well, and Shakespeare began thanking Abraham each day of therapy.

Abraham only smiled. Weeks and weeks of hard, grueling, and painful work ensued, but Shakespeare's progress was phenomenal. His two operations improved the usage of his right leg immensely. He had enrolled in a correspondence school, and his grades were off the charts. The next year, he enrolled in Duke University, thanks to a scholarship offered by the hospital to a deserving young male. Shakespeare was considered family by all the staff, but he was caught completely by surprise the day everyone gathered in the therapy room and presented him with the coveted college scholarship. Shakespeare ran from person to person, thanking each one for their contribution. He was in a state of disbelief. He gave a very emotional speech, and when he finished there wasn't a dry eye in the room … and they hugged all over again.

CHAPTER 10

Since Tom was planning to return Shakespeare's papers on that Tuesday morning after he had finished his column, he buzzed his boss, Don, and asked if he would like to go with him. Don was so delighted he appeared at Tom's office door ten minutes early. When Tom and Don dropped in at the hospital, they found Shakespeare walking up and down the long hall. Tom could sense a nervousness and called his name softly so as not to startle him.

"Hi, Tom," said Shakespeare, trying to act nonchalant, "How do you think I am doing? Today I get to go out into the real world for the first time and I'm afraid I might attract attention."

"Shakespeare, I'm sure that must be quite a challenge, but I also know that you, of all people, can handle it. By the way, I'd like for you to meet an admirer of your writing. This is my boss, Don Curtis; Don, this is Shakespeare you've heard so much about."

"It's nice to meet you, Mr. Curtis. Thank you for coming."

"Shakespeare, it's a real honor to finally meet you. Tom had told me about you and your accident. But I want to talk to you about your incredible gift with words ... and to make you an offer."

"I'm not sure I understand fully, sir."

"Shakespeare, I would like to put you on our payroll for special feature stories while you are in college, and after you have graduated, a permanent position will be waiting, if you are interested."

Shakespeare was overcome. "I don't know what to say. It is so kind of you to want to help me."

"No, Shakespeare, it is not kindness at all, it is actually a selfish move on my part to use your talents before anyone else discovers you," Don said with a smile.

"Thank you, Mr. Curtis, I would be honored to work for you. Tom told me all about you, as well, and I would be proud to call you my boss."

"Thank you, Shakespeare, this is a special day. Welcome to the *Durham Daily News*. Now, you just go out there, in the real world as you call it, and knock 'em dead."

"Thank you, sir." Shakespeare was very humbled by this unexpected opportunity. After Tom and Don left, he offered thanks for the gift he had just received and asked that he be worthy of it.

The day finally came when Shakespeare was to leave the hospital and trade long hours of grueling therapy for college and even longer hours of studying. One of the nurses had invited Shakespeare to stay with her family until he was to enter college in just ten days. He was most appreciative since he had no home, family, or money; he was homeless. Thankfully, his full scholarship would give him at least minimal spending money.

CHAPTER 11

Shakespeare was apprehensive about how the other students would react to his prosthesis and obvious limp. Would they accept him as an average guy, or set him apart as an oddball? As it turned out, primarily because of Shakespeare's warm and caring personality, he was well liked at the university, and nearly everyone had heard his story.

In his junior year, an attractive girl named Janna became interested in Shakespeare and asked a mutual friend to arrange a date. At first, Shakespeare refused, thinking his body would be repulsive to someone like Janna. His friend, Andy, convinced him to go out once and give it a try, so he finally agreed. Shakespeare was a basket case until Janna bounced down the stairs of her dorm, meeting him at the bottom, saying in her teasing tone, "Well, Shakespeare, you're the first one-legged boy I've ever dated." He looked at this direct and unaffected girl and laughed so hard he could barely stop. They connected at once and Janna didn't seem to be bothered in the least that Shakespeare had only one leg … She did care, however, about his mind and his amazing writing ability. It was Janna who shortened his name to Speare, and he did not object, saying Shakespeare sounded much too literary.

They soon became an item, doing everything together. Speare was completely at ease with Janna. They soon became romantically involved to some extent, but Speare knew something was missing in their relationship. He explained his feelings to Janna and they parted ways but remained good friends. Speare went on to date several attractive girls, but there was always something missing. He couldn't explain it, but he knew there was a feeling he was missing, one which he couldn't quite explain but one he felt he had experienced before and wanted again.

CHAPTER 12

Laney's bakery became one of the most successful businesses in the small coastal town. It was quite attractive with its happy colors and drew the tourists as well as the townspeople to its doorstep. Laney was extremely happy doing what she had always dreamed of, until one day when she arrived home after work and found a disturbing note slid halfway under the front door. It read, "YOU KNOW TOO MUCH. IT'S TIME FOR YOU TO LEAVE TOWN." Laney was devastated. Why had this person waited several months to threaten her? What was this secret someone thought she was carrying around? This time she would definitely confide in Mr. Mac and let him know about this threat and the other happenings. She trusted him; he probably would know exactly what she should do. The next morning, after a sleepless night, Laney left the shack early and went straight to the restaurant to talk to Mr. Mac. He was standing behind the cash register and Laney, almost apologetically announced, "Mr. Mac, I have something I need to discuss with you when you have some spare time."

"Why, Laney, we can talk right now. Let's go into my office. I know you so well, Laney. What's troubling you?" And with those words from this gentle giant, the flood came. Apparently, Laney had bottled up all these incidents for a year and a half, denying her fears as foolish, and now that the gates had opened, she couldn't stop. "Oh, Laney, I wish you had come to me sooner. I may be able to help. I don't want to hurt you, but I have known your mother and some of her weaknesses and problems. Occasionally she would confide in me. Once, in fear, she came to me, as you have now, and told me about a threat she had received. I'm sure this influenced the unlimited amount of alcohol she imbibed, which took away any negative thoughts that might have come to her. She became almost a dual personality, and as you know, she could be impossible and hysterical, or she could be caring and loving. Eventually, the first personality almost completely absorbed the latter."

"Mr. Mac, do you know why she was threatened? Is it related to my threat?"

"Laney, I don't want you to worry, but if anything else strange occurs, contact me at once. In the meantime, I will handle this in my own way. Please trust me, Laney. You are like my own daughter."

"I do trust you, Mr. Mac, completely."

"Now, go on to the Sweet Shack and try not to worry. Business as usual."

"Thank you again, Mr. Mac. I love you like a father."

Mr. Mac's eyes glistened with tears as Laney walked next door to open up.

Thankfully, the Sweet Shack was intact, and Laney blissfully began baking, much to her heart's content. One thing she had forgotten to ask Mr. Mac was who owned the shack where she lived. She had been there now, rent free, for more than two years, and her guilt grew more and more. It was her goal to pay the owner for the time she lived there and then buy it. After the lunch crowd had purchased their desserts, almost wiping out the dessert counter, she put a "Back in 10 Minutes" sign on the door and dashed over to the Sea Wind Restaurant. "I'm sorry to keep pestering you, Mr. Mac but I do hope you have the answer to this important question."

"Let me have it, Laney."

The Secret Shack

"Who owns the shack where I live? I would very much like to buy it. Do you know?"

Mr. Mac laughed. "Yes, I do know, Laney, and did you know that it really is a magical shack and so very full of love? Would you like me to tell you the story?"

"If you have the time."

"Many, many years ago, I fell in love with the most beautiful and sweetest girl on the Outer Banks, but unfortunately, she was the daughter of the wealthiest couple on the island. I was considered 'poor white trash,' and Mr. Lovett would not allow his daughter to see me. We were only seventeen at the time. I began collecting scraps of lumber that washed up on the shore and other odds and ends until I had enough to build that lopsided shack in the densest vegetation on the island. Eventually, I added a couple of windows. Leanne would sneak away or say she was visiting friends, and we would meet in the shack where we would spend several hours with each other. Sometimes we would walk along the shore, playing like kids, or go swimming or just talk for hours about our dreams. Mr. Lovett made plans to send Leanne to school in another state to distance her from me. We were so in love. I was going to the technical school across the bridge on the mainland, learning to be a professional chef. My passion was cooking; it was all I ever wanted to do. I knew that eventually I would cook in my own restaurant."

"You did just that, Mr. Mac. May I ask what happened to Leanne, unless you'd rather not tell me."

"No, Laney, I want you to know. Leanne went away to school and did not come home for a full year. We remained faithful to each other and were still very much in love. Our reunion was amazing; Leanne had grown more beautiful than ever. We were so happy. We talked about getting married in two years, knowing her parents would protest vigorously, caring only about her social status, not her happiness. Leanne decided to share our plans with her parents. They became quite angry and threatened to disown her as their daughter. Later, I was informed that Leanne was completely devastated. She ran out of the house and jumped into her convertible, sobbing uncontrollably as she raced down the beach road. In my heart, I knew she was heading for the shack. Do you know the curve in the road near the shack? The driver of the truck that hit her said she was speeding. She came around the curve straddling the center line. It happened so fast; Leanne died instantly."

"Oh, Mr. Mac, I'm so sorry. I never knew."

"No one did, Laney. Of course, Mr. Lovett blamed me. I blamed myself for years, until I realized it was her father who had been so harsh and unfeeling." Mr. Mac and Laney held each other until the tears stopped flowing.

"Thank you for sharing your heart, Mr. Mac. You deserve so much more."

"Laney, I treasure my memories. In that short time, Leanne and I had more than some people have in a lifetime."

"Did you ever date after that?"

"Yes, I've tried several times, but no one measured up to my Leanne.

CHAPTER 13

It was time for graduation! Speare had excelled in all of his subjects, and as a writer, he had won every award and was editor of the college yearbook and magazine. He had several offers from magazines and newspapers, but he signed with the *Durham Daily News*, which had befriended him while he was hospitalized and who tried to help him find his identity.

Speare asked if he could have a week off before beginning his job so he could go to the coast and relax. He had gone twice with friends; he felt drawn to the ocean. The closer he got to his destination, the more familiar the surroundings became. When he crossed over the bridge leaving the mainland behind, he had the most unusual feeling—he felt completely at home. This connection was new for him.

Speare came to the main town but kept on driving as if he knew where he was going. When he arrived at the next town, even though it was much smaller, he pulled over and parked, feeling quite at home. Speare was growing hungrier by the minute, and when he asked for a recommendation, the Sea Wind Restaurant was high on the list. Speare found the Sea Wind Restaurant and, upon entering, his taste buds were immediately activated. Not understanding why, he asked the hostess if he could be seated at the third table from the back. Without hesitating, he ordered slaw, shrimp, hush puppies and a lemon tart for dessert.

"You must have dined with us before, sir."

"No, never."

"But how did you know we had a lemon tart?"

"That's a very good question, but I don't have an answer." Speare enjoyed his lunch while observing some of the people. The gentleman who seemed to know and greet all the customers looked vaguely familiar, as did the cashier. Speare finished his tart and a wave of nostalgia washed over him. On his way out, he asked the friendly cashier, "Do I know you?"

"I don't think so."

"Well. Maybe you have a double."

"Please come back and see us."

Speare's attention was drawn to the attractive shop next door called the Sweet Shack, but he was eager to find a spot on the beach where he could relax and write. After checking in a motel and changing into his swimsuit, Speare drove down the beach road feeling more and more at home. He did not understand this at all. Near the end of the island, he pulled over, unloaded, and headed for the beach. It was a little difficult walking in sand with a prosthesis, he quickly discovered. Immediately, he felt the pull to walk down to the water's edge ... and there he stood. As he stared out over the ocean, he had flashes of a middle-aged man and woman, and then he thought that he heard someone crying. What was happening to him? When he returned to his chair and umbrella, he noticed the dense vegetation, and his curious reporter's mind hungered to see what was hidden within it. Moving in and out of the growth, he came to a group of trees, almost like a room, and again he felt a connection that stopped him dead in his tracks. Moving on, he spotted a little shack, and he almost raced to reach its doorstep. "I know this place," he said our loud. "I know I've been here before." He knocked on the door. There was no answer. He peeped into the windows and fell in love with this charming little shack. He thought, *I wonder who lives here.* Then he saw the handmade table and could almost feel its roughness, now covered by a quaint checked tablecloth. Speare was shaken by these new, unfamiliar feelings.

He began talking to himself. "Could it be possible I have been here before? If only I knew my name, where I came from and what happened. All I know is that I was flown in the hospital helicopter to Duke Hospital from somewhere along the Atlantic coastline after having been nearly killed in a car accident. Tomorrow, I will check with the residents and see if anyone remembers a bad accident involving a convertible and utility truck approximately five years ago." Speare went back to the Sea Wind Restaurant for dinner, planning to ask the presumed owner if he recalled an accident five years ago, but to his disappointment, he learned that Mr. Mac was off for the evening. The next morning, Speare went directly to the main police station but only a young man was there—too young to recall the incident.

"Where is your boss?"

"He is checking on a call down the beach."

"And when are you expecting him to return?"

"Probably about ten o'clock."

"Good, then I'll be back then."

Speare rode through the village, admiring the lovely homes. Suddenly he was drawn to the biggest one of all. As he looked up at the entrance, a flashback of a young boy scurrying out the front door made him quite sad. The boy in his imagination looked so upset. The house definitely looked deserted, so Speare walked up the steps and subconsciously reached for his key. Why did he do that?

He glanced at his watch and rushed to the Beach Patrol office. "Chief, may I have a few minutes of your time?"

"At least introduce yourself," the chief snarled.

"Sir, I meant no disrespect, but that is why I am here. I don't know who I am, and I need your help."

"Well, I certainly don't know you."

"Do you remember the wreck that occurred here about five years ago?"

"You'll have to tell me more than that. With all the teenagers here in the summertime, we have at least one wreck a day."

"All I know is that I was told that a hospital helicopter transported me to Duke Hospital in July of 2001."

"I'd look it up, but all our records for that summer were stolen."

"Would there be someone else who might know?"

"Your guess is as good as mine," the chief said with a sneer.

As he climbed back into his car, Speare not only felt dejection but also was somewhat irritated by the chief's rudeness as well. Maybe tomorrow would be a better day. On the way back to the hotel, he passed the girl on the bike he had seen earlier. She turned and smiled, and he felt a tug at his heart. "What on earth was that? I'm certainly not a teenager," he muttered to himself. He slowed down and watched as she pedaled down the road and pushed her bike into the dense vegetation until they both disappeared from sight. *That's strange*, thought Speare. *This is close to where that shack is.*

The week had passed far too quickly, but Speare was convinced that this place held answers to his identity. He would be back! He wanted to talk with the girl on the bike. There was something vaguely familiar about her.

Monday found Speare at his new job at the paper doing what he loved best—writing. Usually this took precedence over everything else, but the girl on the bike crept into Speare's thoughts until he could barely concentrate on the story he was writing—and he had a four o'clock deadline!

CHAPTER 14

Everyone who came into the Sweet Shack on Monday spoke about the handsome young man with one leg who had been asking if anyone recalled the wreck that occurred five years ago. They agreed he was quite nice, polite and rather quiet. Laney remembered the day it happened, but she never knew those involved. She could only recall that they had been airlifted to Duke Hospital. Laney's heart was heavy thinking about her last day with Daniel. Startled out of her reverie by a muffled sob, Laney looked up and spotted a small girl, maybe six years old, with her nose pressed against the window filled with a plethora of sweets. The little girl was rather shabbily dressed and her hair needed brushing. This was not the first time this child had appeared at the Sweet Shack. Slowly Laney walked toward the door and softly said, "Good morning. It's a pretty day, isn't it?"

"Yes, ma'am, it's pretty," answered the child politely.

"Would you like to come in and pick out a muffin?"

"No, thank you, ma'am, I don't have any money today."

"Well, that's okay. This is your lucky day. We are giving away a free muffin to the first twenty-four people who come in."

"Really? In that case, I suppose I can have one after all."

"Have you ever had a tea party?"

"No, ma'am, but sometimes I pretend I'm having one."

"Why don't you come in and you and I can have a tea party." Shyly, the little girl followed Laney back inside the Shack. "My name is Laney; will you tell me your name?"

"Cassie, my name is Cassie."

"Why, that's a beautiful name. You must have a special mom to give you such a pretty name."

Cassie did not answer. She lowered her head and looked as if she might cry again.

"I'm sorry, did I say something that upset you, Cassie?"

"No, ma'am, I just don't have a mom anymore. She left home when I was four and she hasn't come back, but one day she will."

"Of course she will," Laney murmured, knowing the possibility was highly unlikely. "How old are you now?"

"I'm six."

"Where do you live, Cassie?"

Cassie hesitated and finally said, "I live with some other kids and an old woman who sometimes is not so nice, especially when she drinks too much of her medicine."

Laney was disturbed at this revelation and promised herself to investigate. Laney poured Cassie a cup of lemonade and served her a chocolate muffin, which she devoured as if ravenous. "This is really good. Thank you, Miss."

"I'm glad you liked it, Cassie—and please call me Laney."

"I'd better go or I'll be in trouble."

"What kind of trouble?"

"I'm not allowed to say."

Laney had noticed faint bruises on Cassie's arms and legs and wondered why she had so many. "That's okay, but remember this, Cassie, from now on promise me if anyone ever tries to hurt you, or if you have a problem, or if you need something important, you will come and tell me and I will help you. We are friends now, right? And friends always help each other. Why don't I take you home?"

"Oh no, I'll just walk."

Laney sensed Cassie was afraid the caregiver might be upset, or it was so bad where she lived that she was embarrassed. "I have an idea. Let me take you almost home, and when we're a block away, I'll let you out."

"Oh, Laney, that's a good idea." And she gave Laney a smile that warmed her heart. Off they went and exactly one block away, Cassie cried out, "Stop, we're almost there!" She hopped out and politely said, "Thank you, Laney, that's the bestest time I've ever had."

"Come back in a few days," called Laney. After waiting a few minutes, Laney rode down the next block and saw a small house badly in need of repairs with at least five dirty children playing in a yard filled with trash.

Two weeks passed, and Cassie did not come. Laney sensed that something was wrong. She drove by the house and saw only two children outside until she spied a small figure in a far corner of the fenced-in yard huddled behind a bush crying. Laney slammed on brakes, hopped out, ran over to the fence, and said, "What is wrong?" She could see dried blood and big welts on Cassie's little body. "You come with me right now. I promise no one will ever hurt you again." Cassie ran to the fence and Laney helped her over it and actually carried her to the car. She drove Cassie straight to Dr. Steve's and asked him to examine her. She was afraid and did not want to let go. They were horrified at the extent and the harshness of the punishment given to this fragile child.

"I must report this to Social Services," said Dr. Steve.

"But they will take her away and that will be even more devastating. Why can't she stay with me?"

"I will see what I can do, Laney." Dr. Steve knew Laney had nothing but love to give this sweet child.

Laney picked up Cassie to take her to the car, and Cassie hugged her with all the strength her little arms could muster. Laney went to the shop just long enough to put the "Closed" sign in the window. Then she took Cassie to the shack, cleaned her up, applied the medicine Dr. Steve had given her, and tucked her into bed between the clean, fresh sheets. In a few minutes, Cassie was fast asleep. Laney thought she looked like an angel, and she knew then that she cared deeply for this child.

CHAPTER 15

While at the coast, Speare learned that an undercover operation was located there that involved the Beach Patrol. It was the whispered conversation of nearly every citizen of Goose wherever two or more were gathered. Speare's curiosity was definitely piqued by the rumblings of these townspeople. He was aware that his boss liked to run stories that exposed wrongdoing, so he confided in him and asked to be sent to Goose on assignment. His boss was thrilled that Speare had already sniffed out a possible scoop. In record-breaking time, Speare packed his bags, secured his trusty pen and pad, and was in his car, ready to hit the road. Five hours later, he was at the coast. He went straight to the hotel where he would stay until he had uncovered the covert operation. However, Speare had another mystery he wanted to uncover with as much, if not more, intensity—and the answers to that mystery could be life-changing. Speare was a good young man with great strength and faith. Abraham, the therapist at the hospital, spent a great deal of time with Speare, eventually teaching him about how he was loved unconditionally, all there was to know about receiving blessings, and being a blessing to others. Speare soon understood that God was always present. He developed a sense of peace, accepting who he was. Now, however, in this small beach town, he felt an unrest that had not been present before. And he prayed, "Dear God, I trust there is a reason you brought me here. My life is in your hands. Please show me the way. Your loving servant, Speare."

After checking into the motel, Speare felt his hunger pangs increasing. Since he had driven all the way without stopping for lunch, he was starving. On his way from the Sea Winds Motel, he spotted two Beach Patrol boys stopping and trading off papers, and he wondered what that involved. About halfway to town, he saw a young girl, he guessed to be close to six years old, skipping toward the Sweet Shack. The young lady who came to the door to let the child in was the same young lady he had seen several times riding her bike down the road and eventually disappearing into the vegetation. Speare decided to get out and walk around as if exploring so as not to arouse suspicion. The lady reached down and gave the child a big hug and was rewarded with a brilliant smile. Speare felt disappointed that this child must be the woman's daughter, which probably meant she was married. Nevertheless, Speare walked into the Sweet Shack anyway and pretended to study the delectable baked goods. "I've never seen such a tantalizing array of bakery items," he exclaimed. "Perhaps you could suggest something for me?" He looked directly into the woman's vivid blue eyes. She smiled, but quickly looked away, which reminded him of someone else doing just that. "This sounds like the oldest line, but you remind me so much of someone I knew in my past, perhaps when we're younger."

Laney felt the same way but refused to acknowledge it. "Perhaps I just have a familiar face."

"I feel as though I have heard you speak before."

"I doubt that seriously."

"I'm sorry, I've said too much. How about one of those delectable muffins? You choose."

The little girl was sitting at the table drawing and Speare said, "You have a beautiful daughter."

"Oh, no," laughed Laney, "I would love to claim Cassie as my daughter, but she is my friend."

"Yes, and she is a wonderful artist, too."

"And I'm learning to bake so I can help Laney and she won't have to work so hard," Cassie chimed in.

"Cassie is staying with me for a while." Laney chose a carrot raisin muffin for Speare.

"This is the best muffin I've ever had," he exclaimed. "How much do I owe you?"

"Nothing, it's a welcome-to-our-town gift."

"Then I owe you," said Speare, "and I must figure out a way to repay you. How about having dinner with me tonight? Cassie is welcome too. In fact, I would like that."

"I don't think …"

"Oh, can we Laney?"

"I don't even know your name."

"It's Speare. I'm here on assignment for the *Durham Daily* newspaper, and I'm staying at the Sea Winds Motel at the east end of the beach where all that wonderful dense, vegetation is." There was something in Speare's voice that made her feel safe and unafraid, like a voice she had heard before in her past.

"Tell me where you live and I will pick you and Cassie up."

"Why don't you just pick us up here after I've closed around six-thirty?" Laney always kept a clean pair of slacks and a sweater at the bakery in case she made a mess. She had a change of clothes for Cassie, too. After Speare had gone, Laney questioned her sanity. *I've never gone out with a man, especially someone I don't know. What is wrong with me? I hope I won't regret this but, after all, I am a grown woman.*

Speare was excited. He wasn't really sure why, but he did feel quite comfortable talking with this young woman called Laney. The name Laney resonated with him and he began to wonder if he had known someone in his other life with that same name. He pulled out his trusty journal and found where he had written the name, Laney, even before he was able to communicate. He decided not to mention his discovery to this Laney for fear of making her tense during their time together. Speare thought six-thirty would never come. The hours were moving so very slowly and he was acting like a teenager but did not understand why. Speare knocked on the Sweet Shack door, which was locked, and Laney opened the door holding Cassie's hand. They came outside and she locked the door behind them.

"You ladies look lovely this evening."

"Thank you," Laney responded and Cassie giggled.

"Would you like to have dinner at the Sea Wind Restaurant or could you suggest another place?"

"The Sea Wind Restaurant is fine and you can always count on the food being outstanding." She knew that Mr. Mac would be shocked to see her with a man. As she had expected, all heads turned and conversation stopped when they walked into the restaurant. The people started saying, "Hi Laney." Everyone seemed to know and like her and appeared pleased that she was on a date.

At first, she was embarrassed but Speare sincerely remarked, "It must be wonderful to know so many people and have all of them love you."

"Well, I've lived here all my life."

They were seated and after placing their orders, Speare turned to Laney and said, "There is something I need to tell you, Laney and I hope it won't upset you. My name is not really Speare. About five years ago, I was in a horrible wreck somewhere here on the island and was told that two friends were killed in the wreck. I was airlifted to Duke Hospital and was there and in rehab for almost a year. I didn't know who I was when I regained consciousness and I still have no idea. The doctors say that I suffer from amnesia and hopefully, my memory of the past will return. Because I am a writer, the hospital staff nicknamed me Shakespeare and a girl I dated in college shortened it to Speare. A newspaper reporter befriended me, read some of my material, and showed it to his boss, the editor, who hired me part time. After I graduated, I became a full-time employee."

"That's an amazing story, Speare. There was a wreck near where I live about five years ago and I never knew who the victims were," Laney volunteered, "With so many college kids and summer residents, we often have bad accidents and don't know the people."

"There is one more thing I don't have to tell you but it is who I am now, Laney. I lost my leg in that wreck and the other one was badly mangled but I manage just fine. Now, let's talk about you. Does your family live here?"

"No, I don't have any family."

"I'm so sorry."

"I don't either," echoed Cassie, "but I call Laney family."

"Cassie, you are so precious," she said with tears glistening in her eyes.

"Tell me about the Sweet Shack and how it came to be."

After they had finished the meal, Mr. Mac came over and asked Cassie if she would like to go in the kitchen and watch the cooking and maybe have some ice cream. Cassie was thrilled and besides, she liked Mr. Mac a lot. "Mr. Mac, I would like for you to meet my friend Speare. Speare, this is Mr. Mac, my very dearest friend." Laney began telling Speare how she came to own a business and he was quite impressed.

"How did it get its name?"

"It's a really boring story, Speare."

"But I would like to hear it anyway"

"When I was about twelve years old, a boy my age, one of the summer residents, heard me crying and he consoled me and invited me to a little shack that he had found and fixed up. It was tucked away in the densest vegetation on the island. We became the best of friends and played together every day on the beach and then, we would go to the shack for lunch. Sometimes, I would just sit and draw while he would write. He was a wonderful writer. Sadly, his parents never asked to read his stories, but I loved to read them or have him read to me. He was from the wealthiest family on the beach and they did not want him associating with me, so they left the beach that summer and I never heard from him again. I often wonder what happened to him and if he is happy now. It was very sad for me."

"You cared for him a great deal, didn't you?"

Laney simply nodded her head and then she continued her story, "Shortly after Daniel left, I moved into the shack and began fixing it up as best I could with very little money. Now it belongs to me. I wanted the bakery to be part of the shack and reflect the many wonderful times spent there."

"Laney, thank you for sharing that with me. Maybe before I leave, you will show me the real shack."

"Most people have no idea there is a shack in the vegetation or that I live there. Mr. Mac knows - actually he's like a surrogate father to me."

After they had finished their dinner and talked for a while, they collected Cassie and went back to the bakery. There Laney and Cassie thanked Speare and said they hoped to see each other soon. Laney pulled out her bike, settled Cassie behind her and took off down the road.

CHAPTER 16

Speare had one of the most enjoyable evenings he could remember in a long time. He felt so comfortable with Laney and Cassie. Several times, Speare had a glimpse of the past while Laney was reminiscing. It seemed as though he had been there. *"I hope Laney will learn to trust me enough to show me her shack,"* he thought to himself.

It was still daylight so Speare decided to go to the east end of the island and do more exploring. He pulled into the parking area, got out and began hiking across the dunes to the water's edge. While standing with his foot in the water, lost in his thoughts, an angry wave almost knocked him off balance causing another flashback as if it were déjà vu. "I know I have been here before," he said aloud. "It is far too familiar." "Tomorrow afternoon, I am going to explore the vegetation."

Speare went back to the Beach Patrol station the next day and the chief was still not there. *"Maybe he is purposely avoiding me,"* thought Speare. "Fear of getting caught often caused people to make mistakes. *If I play my cards right and approach him as interested only in finding out about the wreck, he may get careless."* Speare went down the street and watched until the chief returned and then went back to the station.

"Hi Chief, I'm Speare. Remember I was here some time ago and I told you my story. You are a hard man to catch. I was in a bad wreck several years ago and I would like to talk with you and see if you have any recollection of it. I would be most appreciative."

"Sure, come into my office. I'll see if my memory serves me."

"Sir, my name is really not Speare." He went on to explain how he got it and that he is suffering from amnesia, but the doctor thinks his memory will return one day.

"I have no idea who I am."

"I am so sorry," said the chief. "Can you tell me how many years ago this wreck happened?"

"Yes, sir it was five years ago, and I was taken by helicopter to Duke Hospital."

"Well, unfortunately, that happens way too often on the beach road. Let me check my files. That's strange, the year is not in the cabinet. Where could it be and why would anyone want it? I'll do some research and ask around and call you no later than Thursday."

"Thanks, Chief. You're a big help."

As soon as Speare left, the chief let out a huge sigh. "Thank goodness he isn't here for the reason I suspected."

Speare was rather proud of his role-playing and was certain that he had connected with the chief. The fact the file was missing for that year only confirmed there must have been an undercover subterfuge going on at that time. He realized he needed to get to know some of the islanders. Maybe one of them liked to talk too much, would rant on and on about what had been happening. Speare strolled down to the marina where some high-tiders hung out and struck up a conversation with them. He asked if they recalled a bad wreck five years ago. They were sympathetic when he showed them his prosthesis. One old geezer who had been drinking quite a bit said he was walking down the road the day the wreck happened. He said three boys were coming around the curve and there was a power truck straddling the middle line. It plowed into the convertible, but the patrol wrote it up as if it were the kids' fault because he thought they were all dead."

"Did you know any of the boys or where they lived?"

"I know the boy with the car belonged to the folks who used to live in the biggest house on the island. They up and sold their house before the wreck. Uppity folks, anyway. Good riddance, I say."

"Bert, you talk too much," growled one of the other guys.

Speare's palms began to get sweaty "Well, guys, I guess I'd better get back to work before I'm fired. Enjoyed hanging out with you guys."

Speare was excited. Finding out who owned the biggest house five years ago shouldn't be that difficult. He went at once to the Register of Deeds' office. Ten minutes later, he had the owner's name. Now all he had to do was to find out if they had any children and their present address. The Wards' winter home was in Richmond, Virginia. Speare quickly learned the Wards had one son named David Livingston Ward, who would be twenty-three now; Speare was about twenty-three, also. Next, he would secretly try to locate his parents. Either they were deceased or did not care to have anything to do with their only son. At this point, Speare wasn't sure he wanted any answers. Maybe he should talk it over with someone. But whom? The only person he knew casually on the island was Laney. Actually, she had been on his mind all day.

Laney had been catching herself daydreaming all day. She kept reflecting on dinner with Speare and what he had been through in his life and yet he was so positive and pleasant ... and to include Cassie was the sweetest thing. There was something about his mannerisms that haunted her, and even his comment about his pen and paper reminded her of someone in the past. The phone rang; it was Speare.

"Hi, Laney, I just found out some interesting news and I need to talk with someone about it. Would you lend a listening ear and offer some advice?"

"It's Wednesday and I close at one, so come on over and I'll make us a sandwich while you talk, if you'd like."

"Thanks, Laney, you're the best listener I know." When Laney hung up, she remembered one other person who had said that to her: Daniel.

Speare didn't waste any time going over. Laney was just beginning to close. "Go on in the back and have a seat at the table. We can talk while I fix lunch. I'm sorry, but all I have left today is peanut butter and bananas."

"That's fine—that takes me back somewhere in my past."

Speare told Laney what he had found out, but he wasn't sure if he should go to see this family. Suppose they were his parents and had not cared enough to try to find him? "What do you think, Laney?"

"I believe if you don't try something, you'll never know."

Speare sat and thought for a minute, then said, "I feel that someone said that to me a long time ago. I guess I am pretty much a coward and really don't want to know if they don't want me, especially since I'm not a whole person."

"Oh, Speare," Laney said quite emotionally. "You're more whole than most men I know with two legs."

Speare was so moved that he grabbed Laney and gave her a huge warm hug. "Thank you, Laney, for making my day."

They were stunned by the play of emotions from each of them and, unsure how to react, they just stood there for a moment holding each other. Then Laney broke the mood by asking, "Would you like tea or water?"

"Tea will be fine," Speare said, moving away from her. Then he added, "I have an idea, Laney, why don't we go to the beach and play tourist? Besides, you work much too hard."

"Sounds like a good plan to me."

"Do you have to go home and get a swimsuit?"

"No, I always keep one handy."

"Great, let's go. We'll just hang out."

Speare feared what Laney would think when she saw the prosthesis and the badly scarred leg for the first time. Would she be repulsed? But she didn't react. On the other hand, he sure did. "Wow, Laney, you are a knockout."

"You're embarrassing me, Speare."

"I only tell the truth, ma'am. First one in is a rotten egg." And they dashed in like two kids, diving and sneaking up on the other. All of a sudden, Speare went under and came up closer than intended in front of Laney. It seemed like the most natural thing in the world when he leaned forward and kissed her lightly on the lips. They both looked as though they had been stunned. Each said at the same time, "This has happened before. But when?"

"I once played in the ocean with a boy when I was twelve years old and we kissed like that. It took me back to that special moment in my life. I don't know what happened to him."

"Laney, do you agree that this is getting too weird? Everything is beginning to feel like déjà vu."

"Speare, maybe your memory is beginning to wake up and similar things like this have happened to you. I need to go, Speare. Tomorrow is a long day, and I still must bake ten dozen muffins."

"Are you upset because I gave you that little kiss, Laney? I'm sorry if it upset you, but it seemed so natural. Let me take you home then."

"No, I'm fine. I don't live too far from here." She turned and began walking toward the dense vegetation until she seemed to disappear. The moment was almost surreal, as if a fairy tale had just ended.

CHAPTER 17

Speare reached down on the beach towel to gather up the few items they had brought with them and there was Laney's tote. In her eagerness to leave, she must have forgotten it. When he picked it up, there was a jingle, which probably was the keys to the shack. Out of concern, he dumped the contents of the tote onto the towel, and sure enough, a bunch of keys and her cell phone were among several other items, including a seashell with the words, "To Laney, love Daniel" written on it. Speare decided to call Mr. Mac and explain what had happened. He felt he would be invading her privacy if he tried to find her house.

Mr. Mac was impressed with the young man's sensitivity and assured him he would be there in ten minutes. Speare put the objects back inside the tote and waited. He was relieved when Mr. Mac drove up. "I'm sorry I had to call you, but I was afraid Laney would be locked out."

"You did exactly the right thing. She is very protective of her privacy and the shack, as she calls it. Thank you for your good judgment."

As Speare was walking back to his car, he thought he heard voices, but he had seen no one. There! He heard them again! This time they were becoming louder and sounded quite angry. A loud *no* echoed across the dunes and there was silence. Speare stood very still, not knowing what to do, when a man in a Beach Patrol outfit walked over to the parking area where a motor bike was waiting. He saw Speare and said nonchalantly, "Nice evening for a stroll on the beach."

"Surely is," Speare replied. "It is so peaceful I must have fallen asleep and lost track of time. Have a good evening." Waiting until the officer's motor could no longer be heard, Speare walked in the direction the voices had come from. He was shocked to find, lying on the sand, apparently unconscious from a head injury, another young man, also dressed in Beach Patrol garb. Speare found a faint pulse and immediately called 911. He described the area and offered to wait until help arrived. The paramedics came quickly, followed by the Beach Patrol chief and his assistant. The chief approached Speare and asked rather sharply, "What are you doing here? Nobody comes to this part of the beach."

Somewhat irritated, Speare said, "Well, I did and probably will again."

"You will have to come down to the station for questioning since you were the only person in the vicinity."

"I can tell you right now if you hurry, you might be able to catch the Beach Patrol person who left on his bike."

"That sounds like an attempt to cover up, if you ask me. No Beach Patrol officer working for me would ever have committed such a crime."

"Are you suggesting I might have attacked this man?"

"You definitely are a suspect and a stranger to our parts. I'll follow you to the station. Don't try anything stupid."

Speare realized this might be his one opportunity to find out what illegal activities were taking place in the law enforcement agency. He got out of his car and started inside the station when a local news reporter began questioning him. The chief walked over at the same time and blurted out, "Oh, yes, this stranger was at the scene when we arrived. He is our prime suspect at this time."

Speare quietly said, "I've always heard that you are innocent until proven guilty."

"That's enough, get on in the station. This may be a long night."

Speare did as he was told. He was led to a small back room with no furniture except a table, two chairs, and a single light bulb dangling from the ceiling. Speare realized he was being treated like a common criminal but was willing to play along hoping to get an inside scoop. The chief, in his pompous manner, ordered him to be placed in custody.

"I believe I am entitled to one phone call," pleaded Speare.

"Don't hold your breath, buddy. You don't get anything until you come clean."

Speare only said, "Could I have something to eat and drink?"

"Not tonight, buddy".

Speare had endured much more than hunger in his lifetime and he could certainly bear this. Once settled in his cell, he sat down on the bunk bed and began to pray. He knew his strength came from a loving God, and he found peace whenever in communication with Him. He asked for guidance and thanked Him for his presence. He asked that Laney find true peace and asked Him to bless Mr. Mac. Peace came, and Speare slept soundly from exhaustion until he was awakened by loud, angry voices. He recognized the chief's voice, but the other voice was not a familiar one. Now and then, he could pick up words like "botched," "stupid," "no pay," "get it right next time." Speare recorded these words in his mind until he could get a pen and a pad.

Word spreads quickly in a small community, and early the next morning, someone said, "You have a visitor." Speare looked up and saw Mr. Mac standing there smiling.

"How did you know, Mr. Mac?"

"Collect your belongings, Speare, and we will talk over breakfast."

"I'll follow you in my car, Mr. Mac, if that meets with your approval."

"Why don't you do that?"

When Speare arrived at the restaurant, Mr. Mac invited him into his office where they could talk in private. "Have you had anything to eat, Speare?"

"No, sir, not since lunch yesterday."

"Why don't we both enjoy a good breakfast?" Mr. Mac buzzed the kitchen and ordered a hearty breakfast over the intercom. "Speare, you asked how I knew you were being held at the station. Well, the reporter who was questioning you is a friend of mine and he had seen you with Laney and Cassie. He is not a fan of the chief, and he certainly objected to this blatant statement without proof that you were the prime suspect. He also knows that I watch over Laney like a mother hen, so he came to me at once with the news. I assured him you're a good guy."

"I can never repay you, Mr. Mac, for coming to my rescue."

"You may have already or at least started the ball rolling. I'm not at liberty to reveal anything to you, but years ago Laney overheard a conversation between the chief and her mother which frightened her and caused her much pain. Recently, on two occasions, she has discovered someone prowling around her house and once a threatening note was left. I believe it's related to what I just told you. The chief probably thinks Laney will one day reveal what she heard, even though she was only twelve years old at the time. I must admit, however, that I am concerned for her safety."

"Thank you for sharing with me, sir. It helps me to understand her reticence to be close to anyone but you. I do want you to know that a member of the Beach Patrol—or someone dressed like one— came out of the space where I found the man near death. He actually spoke to me, I spoke to him, and he drove off on his motorbike. Then I went toward the direction where I heard voices and the loud 'no,' and found the injured man with blood oozing from his head. He had a faint pulse, thankfully, and I dialed 911 and the chief appeared at the same time. The rest is history. Sir, I woke up last night about two in the morning and heard angry words coming from the front of the building. The chief was yelling at someone whom I presumed was the officer who rode away. The words I picked up were 'botched', 'stupid', 'no pay', and then 'Get it right next time.' The door slammed and there was silence."

"Speare, watch your every move. I believe you are the designated scapegoat, so do be careful."

"Thank you again, sir, I'm so grateful Laney has someone who cares so deeply for her."

"She is a fine young woman, Speare."

"Yes, sir, I know."

Speare spent the rest of the day in his room gathering his thoughts, writing an account of the incident, and trying to sort his feelings for Laney as well as interpreting the quick flashbacks he had experienced this week. Sometimes it was as if his name was on the tip of his tongue, and then it would become muddled. He had to make a decision about visiting the couple in Richmond who had summered in the big house. Mixed emotions controlled his decision to meet the Wards and find out if they once had a missing son. Eventually, he would be compelled to travel down this path. However, for now, the fear and hurt of rejection was more powerful than the desire to have an answer. After talking with Mr. Mac, Speare feared Laney could be in harm's way. He was confident that Mr. Mac would guard her with his life, but he could not watch and protect her all of the time. Speare's gut feeling told him the chief and a man assuming the role of a Beach Patrol officer were the main players in this covert operation. Speare decided his only recourse was to go undercover to observe night and day operations. He was sure the scheme had to do with some of the boats coming into the small port—a perfect place to bring most anything undetected as long as it was relatively small.

CHAPTER 18

Speare drove to the next town and purchased a wig, a moustache, glasses, and shabby looking clothes, including a toboggan. His pants had to be long and loose enough to hide his prosthesis. To add authenticity to his newly acquired personality, he bought an old beat-up bike. Around five o'clock the next morning, he donned his disguise and rode down to the marina where he located a place to sleep, out of sight, but where he could watch any activity going on. Soon a Beach Patrol officer rode up, parked his bike, and strolled over to a boat called *Firefire*, which was docked in slip 22. A rather tough looking guy who spoke with an accent greeted the officer with a familiarity that reeked of longtime friends. The officer looked around nonchalantly before sneaking something out of his pocket and handing it to his buddy. Pretending to check the dock all around, the officer walked to one end and then returned to the *Firefire*. The man on board had a bag marked trash which he passed to the officer. "*Gracias*, officer. You are a good man!" The officer walked over to the trash bin and proceeded to dump out the trash, but he very slyly picked a small bag out and stuffed it into his pants pocket. Hopping on his motorbike, he left the premises and raced toward the station. Speare remained for about ten minutes and then he rode toward the station. Just as he had expected, bike No. 32 was in the bike rack. Speare observed from the pad across the way, and at last, the man came out, followed by the chief. Speare heard him say, "Good job, see ya in three days." Speare made a mental note of that date. The officer took off toward the east end of the island and Speare followed, keeping his distance so as not to arouse suspicion. His leg became very tired. Today was the first time he had tried to ride a bike since having been fitted with a prosthesis. He thought, *I guess there will be many firsts for me.* Speare saw the officer disappear into the vegetation near the same place where Laney had entered several days before. Immediately he felt a jolt of fear that Laney might run into the man or that he might use her house for a hiding place. *Should I follow him or should I call Laney and warn her?* he wondered. *But if I do that, I'll reveal my position. Perhaps I shouldn't jump to conclusions and just wait here instead. Maybe he will emerge shortly. Could he be burying whatever he had into that deep vegetation where he thinks no one goes?* Sure enough, the officer appeared, looked both ways, hopped onto his motorbike, and headed toward town. At almost the same time, Laney pushed her bike onto the road, got on, and headed toward town. She barely glanced at Speare, assuming he was just another beach bum. *I must have on a pretty good disguise,* he thought wryly. Speare had not talked with Laney in almost three days and he realized that he missed this sweet woman.

As Laney rode into town, her thoughts repeatedly went to Speare, no matter how much she tried to put him out of her mind. *Maybe I reacted too strongly to his kiss. I guess I wasn't expecting it, but he was so sweet and gentle. If he finds out I haven't had any experience with men, he might not even be interested in someone so naïve. Should I get in touch with him and say thanks for calling Mr. Mac and asking him to deliver the tote bag I'd forgotten? "What if he is cool to me? Then I can put him out of my mind and move on. Right, as if that might be easy.* Laney pulled up in front of the Sweet Shack and saw a figure run from behind the shack. Without thinking of her own safety, she chased after him, getting close enough to recognize the Beach Patrol uniform. She stopped at once and decided that she should call Mr. Mac about this incident. Why would a Beach Patrol officer choose to remain unseen?

    Laney went inside and checked to see if everything was secure. Since she found no sign of a forced entry, she began to relax.

CHAPTER 19

In the meantime, Speare had returned to his motel room, removed the disguise, and reclaimed his own identity. After seeing Laney, he wanted to be with her more than ever, so he picked up the phone and dialed the Sweet Shack. When she answered, Speare said, "Oh, Laney, it is so good to hear your voice. I have missed seeing you."

"Speare, I'm so glad you called. I've missed you too. In fact, I was just getting ready to call you."

"How about if I get two coffees and come over? Could you spare a muffin?" he teased.

Laughing, Laney answered, "If that's what it takes, the sooner the better."

When he arrived, he gave Laney a quick hug, and this time she hugged him back. After they settled at the table with their coffee and muffins, Laney began describing what happened at the shop just as she arrived. She told Speare the perpetrator had been a police officer, or someone dressed to mimic one.

"Laney, promise you will never do anything that dangerous again!" Speare chastised. "He could have been armed or angry enough to hurt you."

"It was a bit foolish, but I am so tired of being the victim."

"Laney, I want you to try to understand what I'm going to tell you. I cannot give you details, but I want you to know this may be over soon when certain plans are uncovered. So please promise me you will be extra careful and that you will not repeat what I've just said. If you do, I would be placed in a compromising and dangerous position."

"I promise, Speare. Does Mr. Mac know about this?"

"Yes, he is aware something covert is happening, and he may know one of the players. He is such a fine man, Laney, and he loves you so much."

"I know. I'm very fortunate, Speare. But I have an idea. If you're not busy and have the time, let's rent a movie. I'll cook supper and after we eat, we can watch the movie. You must promise not to make fun of my other shack. Even though it's not much to look at, it holds very special memories for me."

"I would never belittle anything you do or have. You should have figured that out by now." Speare was elated. *She must have feelings for me if she is willing for me to visit her shack.* There were no current movies in their little town so they rented an old classic, *An Affair to Remember*.

Laney asked Speare to give her an hour and a half to get ready. She went to the grocery store and after buying fresh corn on the cob, shrimp, items for a salad, and ice cream, she rushed home to prepare it. Speare arrived at the designated meeting place by the road right on time, and there was Laney coming out of the vegetation to meet him. She took his hand, which both surprised and delighted him, and led him in and out, through and under the vegetation to a clearing where a rustic but charming shack stood. "How did you ever find this hideaway?" he asked.

"I didn't. My friend that I told you about came here to write, and one day he invited me to come and see it. I would sit for two or three hours while he would write or read to me. It was wonderful; I still miss it." Speare had an overpowering feeling. "What's wrong, Speare? Are you all right? You're as white as a ghost."

Speare finally spoke. "The strangest feeling came over me. It was as if I had come home. Everything seemed so familiar. I can understand why you love it so—it's so warm and inviting. Thank you, Laney, for allowing me to share your lovely home."

"I grew up with nothing, Speare, so owning this shack is like owning my own palace."

"You are a very special lady, Laney."

Laney placed the food on the table, Speare asked to say grace, and then they devoured a delicious supper while finding so many things to talk about. Speare praised her cooking more than once. After filling up on chocolate ice cream drowned in chocolate syrup, they put the movie in and sat down on the couch to watch. They were enjoying the movie until the accident occurred in the scene where a car hits actress Deborah Kerr and Speare visibly flinched. "Oh, Speare, how thoughtless of me! This must be so painful for you."

"It wasn't that it was painful. It's just ... it was the flashback that revealed a convertible and a power truck coming around a curve straddling the center line. I think I remember that. I'm fine, let's keep on watching. It is one of my favorites. Maybe it will trigger more memories." They got comfortable again and Speare reached over to put his arm around Laney's shoulders. She let out a small gasp, startling Speare. "Does that bother you, Laney?"

"No, but it triggered a memory for me—the last day Daniel and I were together before he left the island with his parents, never to return, and never to write."

"We both have missing links, don't we? Maybe we need to let go." They continued to watch the movie and were both moved when Cary Grant and Deborah Kerr found each other again and learned what had happened. "Is it a coincidence that you're a writer, Speare? Will you read to me sometime? I am an excellent listener."

"No one has ever asked me to read to them before."

"Oh, my, those are the very words uttered to me ten years ago—'And no one ever has read to me before.'"

"I recall words like that, too, Laney. This is all so strange."

The movie ended and Laney said, "I need to call it a night. Tomorrow is a big baking day ..."

Speare didn't let her finish, but instead pulled her gently to him and said, "Laney, this is the nicest date I've ever had. Thank you for that." He tilted her head back and gently kissed Laney, and to his surprise, she returned the kiss. When they parted, they were breathless but grinning like two little kids just given a treat. "Wow," exclaimed Speare. "I'm feeling so blessed right now. I will remember tonight for a long time. I'll call you in the morning."

"Can you find your way out?"

"Oh, yes, I marked the trees," he said jokingly, "in case I decide to come back."

"Good night, Speare, you're the best." She closed the door and watched him find his way through the vegetation until he disappeared from view.

Laney cleaned up the dishes, unaware that someone was observing her every move. She heard a strange noise, instantly closed the curtains, and hurriedly checked the locks on all the windows and doors. Thankfully, Mr. Mac had recently put extra locks on everything. He had also installed a loud alarm and sensor light on her home.

CHAPTER 20

Speare felt so wired that as soon as he reached the motel, he donned his disguise, slipped out into the darkness, jumped on his bike, and rode into town. He went straight to the marina and returned to his claimed homeless space to watch for any further developments. It was a long night for Speare, but thinking of Laney and the flashbacks kept him awake. At three o'clock in the morning, however, a boat pulled into slip No. 22 and Speare could see in the moonlight the word *Firefire* on its side. It was the same boat! The same dark-haired man came out on deck and soon, the same Beach Patrol officer appeared from out of the darkness. He jumped on deck and the two went into the cabin, obviously feeling secure in the dark hours of the early morning. Soon, to Speare's surprise, another man came out of the dark shadows. The Beach Patrol chief wasted no time hopping on board the *Firefire*. Now and then you could hear boisterous laughter, the kind that followed too many drinks, which made them a little careless. Obviously, the noise awakened the caretaker of the marina and a light came on in the building. After looking outside and walking around, he seemed satisfied and went back to bed. This time checking to see if anyone was in view, the chief, holding a bag, quietly slipped off the boat and disappeared into the dark shadows. Fifteen minutes later, the patrol officer sneaked off the boat, reclaimed his motorbike, and pushed it down the road before jumping on it and starting the motor. Speare stayed put for a few minutes, unsure where the chief was hiding out, or whether he had left the premises. Finally, he decided to ride back to the station, keep out of sight, and observe any comings or going … At five o'clock, Speare gave up and went back to the motel, fell across the bed, and was asleep instantly.

The phone rang. Speare jumped up in bed. It was Laney. "Are you all right, Speare?" Speare looked at his watch and saw that it was 11 o'clock. "Shortly after you left, I heard noises outside the shack. I was afraid you might have encountered trouble on the way out."

"Oh, I'm sorry. Laney. No, I'm fine, but I didn't go to bed until five o'clock. I'll explain later when I see you as soon as my meeting with Mr. Mac is over."

"Just be careful."

The chief was a little late coming into work. He said he had been on a stakeout in the adjoining community. Translated by a couple of people in the know, that meant he had spent the night with a woman he had kept hidden for years. The townspeople would quickly add, "because he is not happily married." Only two people knew who the woman was and the real reason the chief kept her out of sight, yet they were unable to do anything about it. Mr. Mac knew the circumstances. The chief had threatened this woman years ago that if she revealed the secret she knew about him, her life would be in danger. With this threat hanging over her, he had held her almost like a prisoner for eight years.

CHAPTER 21

Laney was excited about the bakery workshop she was holding this morning. It had been in the planning stage ever since she had rescued Cassie and the other children. She had made five special aprons for these five deprived young girls. The bell jingled as the door swung open and a voice yelled, "Laney … Laney!" and Cassie ran at full speed into Laney's outstretched arms.

"Cassie, I've missed you and I'm so happy to see you!" Laney said, then she greeted each child, gave each one an apron, and began giving instructions on how to make muffins—Laney's style, of course. Flour was everywhere—on the walls, the floor, the ceiling—nothing was spared. Faces and clothes were snow-white. You could hear happy peals of laughter floating down the street. Finally, it was time to pour the batter into the tins and place them into the oven to bake. What would she do with these active children for thirty-five minutes while they waited? Then she remembered some of the stories Daniel used to read to her. The children were mesmerized and called for more when each story ended. Laney did not see Speare come in, so she didn't see the strange expression on his face when he heard the story she was telling. At one point, as she approached the end of the story, Speare blurted out the ending. Laney looked up in shock and asked, "How did you know that?"

"I'm not sure," answered Speare. "Unless I wrote them."

"If so, do you know what that means? It means that you must be Daniel. Can that be?"

"Tell another story, Laney, and let me see if I know it as well." Laney started the story and Speare finished telling it without hesitating. "Laney, this means I have an identity now, but I've been Speare so long I'm not sure if I can change."

Without thinking, Laney exclaimed, "Daniel, I never thought I would see you again. You never wrote or called. You just disappeared."

"Laney, you called me Daniel. My name is Daniel? What is my last name? I don't think I ever knew."

Laney was happy for Daniel but sad because he still had no recollection of her. Laney suddenly recalled that sometimes Daniel signed his stories with the name "David," and when she asked why, he would jokingly say, "That's my name in my other life."

"Laney, when I researched the family in the big summer house, they had a son whose name was David Livingstone Ward. If I want the truth, my only recourse is to go to Richmond and talk with this couple. The most troubling aspect is why they didn't try to find me—that could not have been too difficult given the circumstances." Too much was happening too fast. He had come to the Outer Banks to uncover his identity, and now that effort was reaching dramatic heights. It was becoming the most traumatic and maybe the most exciting aspect of his journey.

"Laney, I'm so sorry I interrupted this special occasion with the children. They look so bewildered. What can I do to rectify this?"

"Go talk to Mr. Mac; his wisdom and kindness might help you make a decision."

"Thanks, Laney. I'll be in touch."

Laney shivered and thought sadly, *I've heard that promise before and that was the end of the relationship.*

Mr. Mac was the epitome of calmness, and that is what Speare needed and welcomed at this uncertain time of his life. "Speare, why don't you bring me up to date with what has transpired since we last talked?"

Speare quietly related to Mr. Mac everything that had been happening up until the present moment. Mr. Mac immediately expressed concern for Speare and Laney. "Now Speare, I am fairly certain who the woman is, but I don't know what else the chief is involved in. My suspicions have always been smuggling diamonds or drugs. The chief lives far above his present annual salary, which is often the topic of conversation, especially when he acquires another toy or embarks on an expensive undertaking. Our recourse, at this time, is to alert the SBI, tell them what you have observed, and then let them take it from there. What you did was a risky and dangerous way to get a story, but I know that's what you reporters do. Yes, I am still terribly worried about Laney because of her connection with this woman. Let me quickly add, however, that Laney is unaware of this connection. When this is all over, she will need a lot of emotional support—someone she can rely on."

"Mr. Mac, I give you my word that she has and will continue to have my support."

"In the meantime, Speare, promise me you'll let the SBI do all the investigating from now on."

"You have my word."

Speare called the SBI and they arranged to meet early that evening with him and Mr. Mac. When Speare finished telling the SBI his story, the agents thanked him and acknowledged that with his information they would have the ringleader by the next day, if there were no hitches. "We will call in the Coast Guard for backup, but this is all we can reveal to you until it is over," the agent said as they shook hands.

Speare knew that next on his agenda was visiting the Wards in Richmond to determine if they were his parents. What would happen if they refused to see him? Before Speare embarked on his trip to Richmond, he wanted to include Laney in his latest plans.

Laney had arranged for Cassie to visit with her the next day. They would spend time at the beach swimming and collecting shells. They would take time out to get ice cream—Cassie's favorite thing to do—and then go back to the shack to bake cookies so Cassie could take them to the other children. And, of course, Laney would ask Cassie what she would like to do. Laney was so excited. She had grown to love this sweet little girl. She had even dreamed about adopting Cassie but did not know if she, a single woman, would be allowed that privilege. She also feared she didn't have the skills to raise a child properly. No one was aware of Laney's dream, not even Mr. Mac.

Her phone rang. It was Daniel. "Laney, I want to let you know I am going to Richmond this afternoon to face the music. Wish me well."

"Daniel, I will be praying for you. Please let me know the outcome."

"I'll call you, Laney."

CHAPTER 22

Amy, the woman from Social Services, brought Cassie to the bakery. Cassie squealed when she saw Laney and ran to her with a big leap. Amy laughed at this energetic little girl who wore her heart on her sleeve. Laney had arranged for someone to take over at the bakery so she and Cassie could spend the day having lots of fun, something that was almost foreign to this child. Off they went to the beach, one of Cassie's favorite pastimes. They played for a while in the water, and then took time out to search for seashells, and back into the water they would race. Suddenly, it was lunchtime. Laney had prepared a lunch she hoped Cassie would enjoy. Cassie did not disappoint her; she ate until she was stuffed. Laney explained to Cassie that if anyone went swimming immediately after eating, they might get cramps, so instead, they stretched out on the blanket under the umbrella and both went fast asleep. Laney woke up with a start, feeling more rested and relaxed than she had a long time. She saw that Cassie was already up, and she expected to see her gathering shells, but she was nowhere in sight. Laney began walking in the direction they had wandered earlier, calling, "Cassie. Cassie." She got no answer, and when she rounded the bend where she thought the little girl would be, there was no Cassie. "Oh, dear God, I pray she didn't go back into the water alone. Where could she be?" Laney ran as fast as possible to the towel and noticed at once a swath in the sand from the blanket to the top of the hill, as if someone had dragged Cassie through the sand. She followed that path yelling Cassie's name, but the path ended at the parking area. Laney called Mr. Mac, crying hysterically. "Mr. Mac, Cassie has disappeared. She is gone. What can I do?"

"Stay where you are, I'll be there in a few minutes. She probably ran to the shack to get something." Mr. Mac was almost positive the gang involving the Beach Patrol officers was behind Cassie's disappearance, so he immediately alerted the SBI. The agents agreed that, most likely, Cassie had been abducted and was being held as a hostage by these desperate men. Cassie's life was in danger. With the Beach Patrol involved, most likely they had taken her to the marina. Time was critical. Laney blamed herself. How could she have slept through an abduction? The agents tried to calm her by telling her the kidnapers were pros. They had been well prepared. A cloth soaked with chloroform placed quickly over Cassie's nose would render her helpless and certainly unable to speak. *Oh, Cassie will be so frightened,* thought Laney. *Please, Lord, don't let them hurt my precious little girl.* As soon as the SBI had received word of the assumed abduction, they called in the FBI, and the agents wasted no time executing a plan to capture the gang members. Three of their men were sent to the marina—one dressed like a bum, and two others like regular guys getting ready to sail away. Positioned around the marina, out of sight in the vegetation, ten men with assault rifles were ready to close in and/or shoot as soon as they received the signal.

Mr. Mac, feeling that Speare would want to be informed of this latest turn of events, called him on his cell. Speare was halfway to Richmond when the call came.

"I will turn around and come back right now to see if I can help."

"No," answered Mr. Mac, "there isn't anything that you can do. The SBI and FBI have taken over."

"Thank you for letting me know. Tell Laney I'm praying Cassie will soon be returned."

They had removed the tape from Cassie's mouth, and in all of her innocence, she asked, "Why did you bring me here and upset my Laney?"

"Shut up, little girl."

One of the Beach Patrol officers who had a little girl about Cassie's age sharply said, "She's just a child. Treat her kindly if you know how."

Cassie looked at this officer and responded, "Thank you, sir. You are very nice man." She gave him a big hug.

CHAPTER 23

Speare, too, had grown fond of Cassie. He knew how much she meant to Laney. *I feel that I must go back*, he thought. *Not only am I concerned for Cassie, but I am accepted at the marina as a homeless man. I could help; I'd be in a good position to observe.* Speare turned around and headed back. As soon as he arrived, he parked his car in an isolated space, donned his disguise, and nonchalantly made his way to the dock, speaking to the workers he had come to recognize and vice versa. Almost as soon as Speare arrived, he noticed a boat he thought was the *Firefire*, but the name on the side read *Firefly*. Suspicious, Speare walked a little closer, asking for a handout from other boat owners. Sure enough, the man the chief had visited two months before was on the deck of the *Firefly*. Speare wasted no time in calling the SBI and the FBI. The SBI agents were already on their way; they arrived about ten minutes later. Speare casually strolled over to the two men, pretending to ask for a handout. Actually, he was pointing out the *Firefly* and the man with whom the chief had interacted. Speare hastily withdrawn from the scene, ditched his disguise, and rushed to check on Laney and wait with her, hopefully, for the return of Cassie. Speare knew he would find Laney at the shack, hoping that by some miracle, Cassie had just gotten lost while exploring in the vegetation and would find her way back. His gut feeling, however, was that Cassie had been abducted in order to find out what Laney was hiding. Speare found the path to the shack and knocked on the door calling Laney's name. Laney threw open the door and Speare wasted no time in pulling her into his arms.

"Speare, I thought you'd gone to Richmond."

"I got the news when I was halfway there and turned around and came back. I love Cassie, too, and I didn't want you to be alone at such a difficult time."

"Speare, thank you so much for being so considerate, but finding out if your parents are alive must be your number one priority. I'll be fine if you need to go."

"I've been alone for several years; another day or two won't really make any difference."

The phone rang. It was Mr. Mac. "I have good news and I have bad news," he said gruffly. "The good news is that the chief and the owner of the boat *Firefly* or *Firefire*, whichever, were taken into custody with a huge bag of drugs, enough to supply the entire county. The bad news is that Cassie has not been located and the three men refused to cooperate. I'm sorry, Laney, we have just put out an Amber alert and the entire town is searching for her as well as the SBI and FBI. Who knows, she may have escaped and is hiding out somewhere, too frightened to come out. We'll call you the second the information is forthcoming. Laney, I know you must remember what comes first at times like this, right. Don't lose faith, and always let God be in control."

"Thank you, Mr. Mac, for reminding me that a greater power than I will look after Cassie. Won't I ever learn that lesson?" moaned Laney, chastising herself.

Neither Laney nor Speare were the least sleepy, nor could they stop pacing or looking out the window. Finally, Speare pleaded with

Laney to go to bed and rest for a while. He promised to awaken her with the least glimmer of news. Laney fixed a pot of coffee so Speare might stay awake; however, eventually when he sat down on the sofa, he was out like a light in a few moments. The jarring ringing of the phone awakened Speare; it was Mr. Mac again.

"Speare, things are not looking good. Is Laney within earshot? The beach towel we assumed they used to wrap up Cassie with was found in the trunk of the chief's car. We hope this means she is still on the island. Don't mention this to Laney; she already blames herself."

"Thanks, Mr. Mac. Please keep in touch."

Laney came running out of her bedroom demanding, "Who was that? Was it about Cassie? Have they found her?"

Speare spoke in a firm voice. "Stop, Laney, stop and breathe. Take a deep breath, get control of yourself, and then I will tell you about the phone call."

Laney fought to calm down. "I'm sorry. It's just that I'm so scared for Cassie."

"First, let me get us both a cup of coffee, and then we will sit on the sofa and talk calmly." Speare proceeded to relay the information Mr. Mac had shared, and, as he expected, Laney began to sob uncontrollably.

"It's all my fault, it's all my fault," she choked.

"Laney, you must stop blaming yourself. The person who is responsible most likely used chloroform on Cassie or she would have cried out. There was no way you could have prevented it from happening. They are pros. You are a sweet, loving person."

"Thanks, Speare. I know you're right but I keep thinking, 'what if?'" By then it was five-thirty in the morning and darkness was just beginning to fade.

Something hit the door hard enough to make it rattle. Looking out the front window, they could only see a large white bundle near the door. Laney grabbed Mr. Mac's old pistol from its hiding place and gave it to Speare. As he yanked open the door, he heard a whimper coming from the bundle. He did not see or hear anyone, but, to be on the safe side, he told Laney to call Mr. Mac and remain on the line with him. Cautiously, Speare opened the bundle, and there was Cassie, so frightened she could not speak.

"Oh, Cassie, I am so glad you're back home," he said, giving her a hug, but she only stared at Speare. "Tell Mr. Mac to send the paramedics; Cassie is here, but she's been drugged or she's in shock."

"My poor baby," Laney moaned, holding the girl and rocking her back and forth. It seemed to take forever for the medics to arrive but it was only twenty minutes. After examining Cassie, they determined that she should be re-examined and tested for any sedatives and perhaps see a child psychiatrist skilled in dealing with abducted children.

"May I ride with her?" asked Laney.

"Are you family?"

"She doesn't have any family and Social Services is allowing her to visit with me."

"In that case, it should be all right to waive the rule."

Speare agreed to follow, after locking up. As he picked up the towel, a piece of paper fell to the ground with words printed boldly in red. "NEXT TIME SHE MIGHT NOT BE SO LUCKY AND YOU MIGHT BE THE ONE TO PAY THE PRICE." Speare shivered at the double threat and wondered what Laney could possibly know that made this person so desperate. He stuck the note in his pocket, locked up, and then hurried to the hospital.

Laney was waiting impatiently at the hospital entrance. "Speare, there's no change in Cassie. She is still staring into space, showing no emotion. Right now, she's having a CAT scan to rule out the possibility of a head injury, and several other neurological tests. After an evaluation, the proper treatment will be determined. Speare. I am so afraid for that sweet little girl."

Mr. Mac came in only a few minutes later to offer his support.

Laney excused herself to go to the ladies room. Speare took this opportunity to tell Mr. Mac about the note he had found in the beach towel Cassie had been wrapped in. "Mr. Mac, will you let the FBI know about this? Laney is walking on eggshells right now, and I don't believe she can handle anything else. Besides, I think I know who one of the officers in the gang is. Remember the day I found that man who had been beaten up. I'm pretty sure this guy is the officer I talked to that day. He's one of the main characters in this scheme of things. If he could be found, identified, and interrogated, we might be able to eliminate the threat to Laney. There's no doubt in my mind that I can identify him if he can be found. If we only had an artist who could sketch a composite picture, I could describe him. He was my height, five feet eleven and a half inches, and weighed about one hundred and sixty-five pounds. He had an olive complexion, green eyes, somewhat slanted, with bushy dark eyebrows. His hair was black and thick but covered with the BPO baseball cap. He had a Roman nose, lips that were rather thin, a square face, and chin with an indentation. I would guess he's about forty-five and he was quite fit."

Laney returned to the room and asked, "What can I do?"

"Wait a second. Laney, you said you draw. Draw this description of the police officer. You tell me in what order you want me to describe each feature."

"I never had lessons, Speare, I just draw for my own enjoyment."

"Please try, Laney. We can always call in an expert later, but now time is everything."

"Okay, but don't laugh at me. I'll try. But I need a pencil and paper. Tell me the shape of his face first."

Laney drew, Speare guided, until by trial and error and Laney's amazing hidden talent, Speare yelled, "You did it! That's amazing, Laney, the likeness is absolutely amazing. You are amazing. We'll get this sketch to the SBI at once and let them circulate it. I'd know this man anywhere." Speare gave Laney a big hug, picked her up, and twirled her around and around. Putting her down gently, he said, "When this is all over, we are going to discuss what you plan to do with your extraordinary talents. For now, our concern is helping

Cassie return to the precious, carefree little girl we know and love so much."

The attending psychiatrist, Dr. Ross, came out of Cassie's room and asked to speak to someone named Laney. Laney jumped up quickly. "Is Cassie all right?"

"At this time, she is still in a withdrawn state, brought about, as you know, by the trauma she has experienced. Unfortunately, we do not know everything that has happened, so we do not know the depth of the trauma. The fact that she is calling your name, however, is somewhat encouraging. It indicates she wants to connect, that she is reaching out. I would like you to go in and talk to her, but you must not bombard her with questions. Simply talk about things you might have done together that she enjoyed. Tell her that you love her and suggest what you will do when she recovers. Can you handle that without getting emotional?"

"Yes, doctor, I can do anything you suggest if it will help Cassie."

Dr. Ross smiled and thought to himself, *With a friend like Laney, I have a feeling Cassie will recover.*

Laney entered the quiet room and burst into tears when she saw Cassie sitting in bed staring into space, her face devoid of all emotion. Laney approached Cassie's bed slowly and softly called her name. "Cassie, it's Laney. I am so glad to see you. We were so worried, and now you're back home, which makes me very happy." Cassie neither blinked nor smiled. Laney gently reached for Cassie's hand; it remains lifeless. Laney tried talking again. "As soon as you feel better, Cassie, we can have some more of your favorite cookies and muffins. Would you like that?" There was still no response. Laney was not going to give up, so she began singing a little ditty she often sang while baking. To her astonishment, Cassie began singing the song, but she did so with that same blank expression and without moving her body. When Laney finished, she hugged Cassie and said, "I didn't even know you knew the words to my silly little ditty. That was wonderful! Maybe we can sing more later." Again, there was no response. The nurse entered and kindly suggested to Laney that she had visited long enough. Cassie needed her rest.

Walking back to the waiting room, Laney sensed someone staring at her, but when she turned to look behind her, a male nurse turned abruptly but not before Laney saw his eyes and knew at once they were the eyes she had sketched. She could never erase that evil look. Without thinking of the danger, Laney quickly changed direction and followed the nurse. Realizing that Laney was catching up with him, he began running to the next exit. Laney yelled out, "Stop that nurse, he is an evil man!" And she kept on running. Someone called security and at the same time two male nurses tried to block the door, but the man turned and headed for the stairs. Somehow, he eluded everyone. Laney was in tears when she returned to the waiting room where Mr. Mac and Speare were chatting, oblivious to what had just occurred. They were sure she was upset because of Cassie's condition, but Laney finally regained her composure and explained what had happened.

"Are you positive it was the same man?" Mr. Mac questioned.

"If my sketch is correct, it could be no one else."

He had escaped again. Mr. Mac notified the SBI and an APB was sent out for this dangerous man wanted for murder, last seen in the Dare County Hospital. So far, the sketch did not match any of the criminals on file. Speare insisted it was a perfect likeness. Security was tightened on the fourth floor where Cassie was staying.

Laney, however, had a big problem—her new business was being neglected; she did not want a guard, and she insisted on being with Cassie during visiting hours.

The interrogators had been unable to break the chief's silence. He refused to speak about anything. The other man who owned the boat professed to speak only Spanish. Even when they brought in a Spanish interpreter, he refused to talk. They knew they were safe as long as the unknown Beach Patrol officer remained unidentified. Where could this man be? He had completely vanished, or maybe he was a man of many disguises. The one giveaway, which the man did not realize, was his distinct and outstanding eyes. The chief was so confident he would soon be free that he was boasting to all the other prisoners. Money was no object! In his one allowed phone call and his domineering manner, the chief had ordered his wife to bring the one million dollars in bail money and to hurry up. Poor Isabel had enjoyed the things the chief's money could buy, but she had put up with his abuse and demeaning treatment in order to qualify. At first, she thought about ignoring his request and leaving him behind bars, but, in retrospect, she was certain her life would be worthless if he found another way to gain his freedom. She did possess one ace in the hole, though, and only she and one other person had this information.

Speare continued to place his trip to Richmond on hold. His top priority at this time was Laney and Cassie. Mr. Mac had pleaded with Laney to move into the apartment above the restaurant until the Beach Patrol officer was apprehended, but she declined. Laney feared that the shack would be destroyed unless it was occupied by someone who would fight to protect it. She would use the gun Mr. Mac had given her if necessary to keep her home intact. The shack was the only real home she had known and the one place that held happy memories from her earlier years. It was inappropriate for Speare to stay with Laney and Mr. Mac had a business to run, so what was their alternative? They decided Mr. Mac would spend the night and Speare would stay during the day. Laney finally agreed to what she referred to as a baby-sitting arrangement. The next morning, Speare arrived and Mr. Mac accompanied Laney to the Sweet Shack, where she baked for two hours before time to open. Her mind, however, was in the hospital room where Cassie continued to stare into space. Laney was eager to try to get a second response from her, either by singing or talking about familiar things. If these failed, she had one more idea she was holding in abeyance. At nine-forty-five, Millie, one of the waitresses Mr. Mac trusted, came over from his restaurant to stay at the bakery long enough for Laney to get to the hospital during visiting hours. Laney walked into Cassie's room and was surprised and pleased to find her sitting in a chair, but she had the same glassy stare. Laney began talking with her, but to no avail. She tried singing, but neither brought a response. Without weighing the circumstances, Laney softly said, "Cassie, would you like to come and live with me in the shack?" At first, there was no reaction, and then Laney spied tears rolling down Cassie's cheeks. "Oh, Cassie, you would make me so happy. I love you so much." With that expression, Cassie began sobbing uncontrollably, so loudly that the nurse came in to assess the situation.

As she entered the room, Cassie cried out, "Laney, do you really mean what you just said?"

"Yes. I do, Cassie. You are truly special to me."

All the staff heard the good news, and they were ecstatic. The attending nurse sent for the psychiatrist, who pronounced Cassie back to normal after a series of tests. Then it dawned on Laney that she must apply for guardianship or adoption if Cassie were to live with her. She then proceeded to try to explain this as best she could to Cassie. "I'll ask the social worker if you can stay with me while the process takes place."

"Laney, thank you, thank you, thank you, I love you soooooo much."

"Visiting time is over, and I must sell some muffins at the Sweet Shack this afternoon. I promise to come back for the two to two-thirty visitation," Laney said, giving the little girl one last big hug. "See you after a while, Cassie."

CHAPTER 24

While walking to the Sweet Shack, Laney was so lost in planning where Cassie would sleep that she failed to notice a man following at a distance. He was dressed in khakis, a denim shirt, Docksiders, and wearing sunglasses. He looked like your average tourist casually walking around their little coastal town. It dawned on Laney that Speare might not want to have a little girl around if he should ask her for another date. *Oh, dear. What have I done? I didn't think about the circumstances, or the responsibility, or the expense, or the confinement, or any of the consequences of having a child live with you. I just wanted to make Cassie well again,* she thought. And then aloud she said fiercely, "And I have no regrets!"

The town square was across the street from Sweet Shack and the ocean was beyond that. Laney entered the shop, paid Millie, and thanked her for her time. As soon as Millie left, she walked over to the window and stared at the water. Laney understood the meaning of alone. All of her life she had been alone with no father and alone with no mother most of her years. She had no one to advise her, to talk with, to hold her close, no one to encourage her, to praise her, to teach her right from wrong. And no one to say, "I love you." The vastness of the ocean was a constant reminder of her loneliness, of the danger of being alone, but she loved the water and one beautiful memory of that special summer when she did not feel alone. Her thoughts turned to Speare, and she wondered if this impulsive decision would push him away. Imagining life without Speare almost brought her to her knees. The weakness overcame Laney. She felt as if the breath had been sucked from her insides. What was wrong with her? Speare had made no commitment. It was the hope within her that motivated her waking hours, provided her with energy. and brought life to her eyes. Silence must be her response for she had not been invited to share what was on her lips and in her heart and mind. Without warning, doubt assailed Laney with what ifs ... What if Social Services deemed her too young? ... What if her resources were inadequate? ... What if her background was rated undesirable? ... What if ... What if? But most importantly, what would happen to sweet Cassie? "Lord, I don't care about me, but I ask you to please give Cassie a good life," she prayed. "And if it's with me, I will know that I've been blessed. Amen."

A man entered the bakery, but when Laney turned to welcome him and ask how she might help, the hairs on her arms stood up. What was wrong? The man had done nothing to threaten her. "I'll have one of those carrot raisin muffins," he said. "That should do it." In addition, he tossed a $100 bill on the counter.

"I'm sorry, sir, but do you have a smaller bill? I don't keep much money in here."

"Sorry, lady, guess I'll take my business elsewhere. I only came in here because a friend said you were a hot number and I should check you out."

Laney was so insulted and angry, but she managed to remain outwardly cool as she responded with assurance and authority. "Mister, I don't know who would give you such false information, but please accept this muffin as a gift and leave immediately since neither of you are welcome. And don't bother to come back."

Mr. Mac walked in as the stranger was leaving. Laney was shaking all over. She told Mr. Mac about the conversation, and Mr.

Mac called the SBI number. He followed the man as he walked toward the beach where he suddenly hopped on a bike and rode down beach road. To be on the safe side, Mr. Mac alerted Speare about Laney's incident and suggested he be on guard.

CHAPTER 25

It was noontime and, tired of staying inside, Speare walked down to the beach for a brief break. A storm was predicted for later in the day and the ocean already was revealing its angry side, foaming at the mouth. Speare stood ankle-deep in the raging water, gazing toward the horizon. A vision of a young girl playing in the water became real, but only for a moment. What did this recurring picture mean? Simultaneously, abandonment came to mind. Did his parents not put forth any effort to find him? Maybe they did not want a son with a missing limb. The thought flashed through Speare's already troubled mind. Perhaps he had been a failure, a child who brought embarrassment to the family name. He had no recollection of anyone ever loving, nurturing, encouraging, or praising him. Why couldn't he remember something, or just anything? If only he could relax and enjoy more time with Laney, maybe he would have more flashbacks. She was so comfortable to be around, he thought, and was constantly praising and nurturing him. What was it about this young woman that always made him feel like a real man? She was so un-assuming. There was no pretense—she was so herself, but who was she? If he ever had a child … but who would marry a man like him? Women would probably look at his body in disgust.

Laney never even blinked when they went swimming and his body with its missing limb and ugly scars were exposed. He needed—no, he wanted to spend more time with Laney. Laney's presence somehow offered a connection, though still indefinable, to other times and events. Speare decided to tell Mr. Mac he would stay on until midnight in order to visit with Laney. She walked to the shack and found Speare preparing supper, looking rather comical in one of her aprons. He stopped stirring long enough to give her a welcome home hug. "What's going on?" asked Laney. "Surely you have more important things to do."

Speare smiled. "After enjoying this amazing and delicious supper which I have prepared, we will have a little talk."

"Fine," responded Laney, convinced that she knew what Speare wanted to discuss, but she was too afraid to ask. Laney, barely recalling what she had consumed, expressed appreciation to Speare for his thoughtfulness and then stated firmly, "I'll wash the dishes later."

"Very well," Speare relented. "In that case, come and sit beside me on the sofa." Laney joined him on the sofa with a heavy heart and purposely sat near the opposite end. "Is something wrong, Laney? You have been quiet all evening."

All during the meal, Laney had felt Speare was poised to give her bad news that he would soon be moving on. "With all of the events and stress of the last few days and trying to run the Sweet Shack, I must admit to being just a little tired."

"You are such a good and strong woman, Laney. I am so glad that our paths crossed … And Cassie is a very fortunate little girl. Mr. Mac told me what you're planning."

"I don't want her to grow up like I did," said Laney quietly. "I only pray that it was the right decision."

"You are a caring and sensitive woman, Laney. I am sure you will be a good mother for Cassie, but there's another matter I need to discuss with you. You may not like it. Two items are foremost on my mind lately—regaining my memory and discovering my birth parents. The first one involves you. It has been evident on both occasions when I kissed you—a flashback would occur of a younger boy and girl, and it was so real. If you won't find it repugnant or demeaning, I would like to intentionally re-enact those kisses as often as is necessary to try to bring me back to reality."

"I see," muttered Laney, so shocked and disappointed she found it difficult to answer. Finally she said, "Sure, anything that's good for the cause." But she ran to the bathroom, closed the door, and burst into tears. So now she had her answer. Speare was being nice to her for the sole purpose of hoping to regain his memory. Laney splashed cold water on her face, patted it dry, quickly straightened her shoulders, and walked over to Speare with her usual cheerfulness. "I'll be honored to be your guinea pig, Speare." He never noticed the significance of that statement. "You need your rest so perhaps we should get started."

Laney tensed when Speare moved closer and put his arm around her shoulder. Her heart was breaking; it seemed such a mockery of what she felt. He then turned her head toward him, tilted her chin, and gently touched her lips with his. Laney tried hard to steel herself against his touch, but instead her heart melted and she responded. Speare, too, was unnerved by the kiss and deepened it until Laney pulled away and gasped. With an edge to her voice, she quickly gained her composure and said, "Let's get on with the experiment."

"Are you sure you're up for it?"

"Oh, I'm fine. Anything to help a friend."

Speare was finally beginning to sense that Laney was not behaving in her usual positive and gentle manner. He wondered, *Have I done something wrong?* But out loud he just said, "Well, if you're sure you're okay, let's try again." Speare pulled Laney into his arms and proceeded to give her another kiss. Again, Laney could not help but respond. For a moment, she forgot that this was an experiment and put her arms around Speare, giving back as much as she had received. Speare forgot as well. He felt such tenderness for this girl that he didn't want to stop. Laney pulled back, hearing Speare murmur lovingly, "Oh, Laney."

"Did you say something, Speare?"

"Yes, I said how beautiful you are, inside and out."

"Thank you, but I am so sorry this replay hasn't helped your cause."

"Somehow the cause, as you call it, doesn't seem so important anymore, Laney. I find that being with you far overshadows the mystery of who I am, but I'm not sure if anyone could be comfortable with me not knowing my identity. I could be a serial killer, rapist … I could be married, a father, a first-class jerk. That's why it is so important to find out."

"Speare, I know you, and I feel as if I have always known you. In my heart, you can be none of those things. You are a fine, upstanding, and considerate gentleman." Laney wanted to add, "And I love you," but knew she could never risk saying those words.

"One day soon, I will go to Richmond and at least learn whether or not I have parents who lived there."

The man in the khakis slipped into a cabana on the beach, donned an SBI uniform as his disguise, and came out to retrieve his bike from a bike stand in the square. His destination was the east end of the island, and his intention was to get the information from Laney that he was confident she possessed. He had been offered an incredible amount of money to secure this information, and he was hungry for money. This time, nothing would stop him. No one would stand in his way.

Laney was emotionally drained. She told Speare she was too tired to continue the experiment.

"Perhaps we can work on it tomorrow after work down by the ocean's edge where you have had other flashbacks."

"Great idea, Laney, you're right, when we played in the water, several images popped up. Thanks, I'll give you a call later in the day to see how you're feeling." Just as Speare started to leave, the lights went out.

"Speare, don't go," Laney cried out. "Something must be wrong. My backup lights are off, too."

"Laney, give me your hand. Someone just opened the back door. Be quiet, and we'll slip out the front door quickly. Just follow me." They exited undetected, and then Laney led Speare into the vegetation where she had hidden as a child. They dropped into the indentation in the sand, and Speare held Laney close. He thought he heard someone crying until he realized it was a flashback.

"Oh, my God, I've been here before. I'm sure of it," he whispered to Laney.

"Why do you think that?"

"Someone was crying, and I found them and took them to my little house. It was a young girl and I was the young boy."

"What are we going to do, Speare?"

"Right now, I'm calling Mr. Mac to ask him to contact the SBI to send someone out to find out who is inside your house. Then we're staying here—until daylight if necessary, when we can see if it's safe to come out."

It was such a small space, they had no choice but to snuggle and wrap themselves around each other. Laney thought, *I can stay this way forever.* Speare reached down, found Laney's lips, and they both drowned in the kiss. When they parted, neither could speak, nor did they want to break the spell. The spell was broken, however, when shots rang out and bright lights were seen waving back and forth through the vegetation. The silence was shattered when Laney heard Mr. Mac call her name. She did not want to ever move from this magic space. Speare, shocked at the emotions he was experiencing, managed to say gently, "Laney, we will talk later." Then, louder, he called, "Over here, Mr. Mac!"

"Keep on talking so we can find you."

"Over here, Mr. Mac, you're almost on top of us."

"What happened? Who was in my house?"

"Let's go back to your house now where we can all be comfortable, and then I'll tell you the entire story."

Speare fixed a pot of coffee for Laney, Mr. Mac, the SBI officers, and himself and they gathered around the kitchen table to bring Laney up on all that had transpired. "But I heard a shot," exclaimed Laney. "Was someone killed?"

The head SBI man jumped into the conversation and quickly explained, "No, no one was killed, but he was injured and was taken to the hospital under guard. He is the last piece of the puzzle we have been trying to capture for a long time. He holds all the key information that will reveal the chief's involvement in this mammoth operation. Actually, this man was so frightened that he offered to tell everything. Laney, you are safe now, so no more worrying that you or Cassie will be harmed. I am going to excuse myself now, go to the station, and enjoy interrogating this evil man. Mr. Mac can fill you in on anything else you might want to know."

"Thank you, officer," Laney said appreciatively.

CHAPTER 26

"Laney, what I must tell you will come as a huge shock that, hopefully, could turn into a joy later on," Mr. Mac began, reaching across the table to hold Laney's hand and looking seriously into her eyes. "First, I'm sure you want to know why you have been a victim—followed, threatened, Cassie abducted, and your home invaded, among other actions. Can you remember when you heard your mom and the chief arguing and the chief threatened your mom if she dared mention what she knew?"

"Yes," Laney replied, "but more vividly, I recall her threatening me, which was more frightening, and that's when I left home and moved into this shack. To have my own mother threaten me, in addition to her other problems, was the most hurtful and demeaning action a daughter could receive."

"Laney, I know that what I'm going to say will not take away the pain or right the wrong, but it might help you forgive. You see, you only heard part of the conversation. The chief not only threatened to hurt your mother, but he promised to inflict something horrible on you, maybe even kill you. So from then on, your mother had to do everything the chief demanded. In fact, Laney, this next information

I am going to share with you will no doubt, be a great shock to you, but you must know that your mother is still alive."

"Oh, my dear God in heaven, where is she?"

"It's not a pretty story, but she has been locked in an apartment in the next town for all these many years, at the beck and call of the chief. She has never stopped loving you, Laney. This is a lot for you to absorb all at one time, but if you decide you would like to visit her, just let me know."

Laney could barely breathe. "I need to think this through and pray about it. It's all so confusing."

"Take all the time you need. Your mother understands if you don't want to have any kind of relationship with her, However, when you feel strong enough and would like to hear the rest of the story, I will tell you what your mother has endured in order to protect you."

All of a sudden, Speare blurted out, "Laney, you must be the young girl I heard crying in my flashback. Could I possibly be the young man who found you and invited you to the shack? If that is true, that would explain why each time I am here, I have this sense of coming home, plus this incredible urge to write and read aloud to someone."

Laney gasped when she heard Speare's words because they brought back such wonderful memories. But not wanting to give him false hope, she chose her next words cautiously. "Speare, let me tell you what I experienced at age twelve and at age eighteen with a young man named Daniel." When Laney finished her story, for a brief moment, there was this complete, ear-shattering silence, broken only by the sound of Speare crying.

Through his tears, almost as if he were in a trance, he said lovingly, "I was lonely and you took me in. I was hungry and you fed me by showing interest in my writing. I was sad and you taught me how to find joy. Then I died and now I am alive. I was lost and you found me, giving me hope." As the words trailed away, he paled and looked panicky and frightened.

"What's wrong, Speare?"

"There's a white truck coming around the curve and it's in the middle of the road. Oh my God!" He began to cry out with pain. "Someone was with me—two of my close buddies. What happened to them? Were they killed?"

Mr. Mac walked over and put his arms around Speare like a father would. He just held him briefly before speaking. "Speare, two young men were with you, but they did not make it. I am so sorry. But you revealed something else that was a lie—the driver of the power truck told the cops that a car full of teenagers came around the curve straddling the center line and ran into him. He was not charged with any wrongdoing. He simply walked away."

Laney gently embraced Speare, murmuring to him, "Daniel, from now on, everything is going to be all right. You are healed. Though painful at first, you have been blessed with the gift of remembering."

Speare pulled Laney into his arms and felt a peace unlike any he had ever known. Mr. Mac gave them each a hug, saying he was going to leave but telling them to call for any reason. He intuitively knew they had so much to discuss. Before he went out, however, Laney confided, "I would like to hear what you have to say concerning my mother. I need to know. When you have time to tell me the rest of the story, I'll be available.

"If you'd like, Laney, I can come by the Sweet Shack tomorrow after you close."

"Thank you, Mr. Mac. That would be good."

As soon as Mr. Mac was out of sight, Speare grabbed Laney, spun her round and round, and then claimed her with a passionate kiss. "You have no idea how long I have wanted to do that again. I've thought of nothing else."

"Oh, Speare, I have felt the same way. You have been in my thoughts every second." Finding joy in simply holding each other, Laney broke the silence with words of concern she had been harboring for fear Speare would be unwilling to share in what she was planning. "Speare, I want to talk with you about my plans with

Cassie. When she was in a catatonic state and I exhausted every trick, tool, and effort to break that spell with no success, I promised she could come and live with me. She reacted immediately. You have never seen such joy on anyone's face—it lit the entire hospital room. I did this, Speare, without thinking about my limited funds, my small and most likely unacceptable living space, my job, my lack of parenting skills, and the effort it takes to prove I am worthy and responsible."

"Of course you're worthy, Laney."

"No wait, Speare. It's not that simple. I do love Cassie. She is adorable, bright, lovable, and so very special, but I acted impulsively. What if I should react like my mom treated me?"

"Laney, stop it right now. You are not your mother, and besides, your mother was under the influence of alcohol. You are a kind, loving, giving, bright, and hard-working young woman. You will be a wonderful mother."

"But I am so young."

"That's even better—that's only more reason for you to understand and relate to Cassie. If it is what you truly want, Laney, then go for it! Cassie is special and so easy to love, and it's pretty obvious how much she loves you."

"Thank you, Speare, you always help me put my worries into perspective." But deep inside, Laney was worried about the things Speare had left unsaid. *Will it keep Speare from wanting to spend more time with me? Will it prevent him from wanting to become more serious with me? But why should I worry when Speare has never even told me that he loves me. Maybe he sees me as only someone who could help him find his identity.*

Speare interrupted her thoughts when he announced his own plans, "Laney, I plan to go to Richmond tomorrow to see, once and for all, if the Wards are my true parents. I am uncertain as to where that will lead. I suppose time will tell."

Laney was crushed when he didn't mention her or their relationship. Obviously, she was not included in his future.

Maintaining all of her courage and control, she managed to say, "Speare, you must be agonizing about this problem. I do hope you will find the answers you want on this trip. I'll be praying for you."

"You are a sweetheart, Laney. I should go now and get some sleep if I plan to hit the highway at seven o'clock in the morning. Good night, sweet lady, I'll call you." And, as he walked out and Laney closed the door, she felt as if Speare had exited her life again with no promise or assurance of returning.

CHAPTER 27

By the time the door closed, she felt the emptiness, the darkness, and the aloneness that had been such a big part of her former life. Like a zombie, she walked to the sofa, sat down, and stared into space until exhaustion took over and she finally fell asleep. After several hours, Laney stirred and was surprised to see the morning light breaking through the darkness. At first she wondered why she was on the sofa, but then she was reminded of Speare's leaving. Trying to put on a brave façade, Laney said to herself, "I know that life goes on, and now I must turn my thoughts to Cassie and my promise to her. She doesn't need to be hurt because I'm hurting. Today I will start the process." Laney got up, feeling like an old lady and very sad but determined to regain her positive, cheery attitude.

A shower, clean clothes, and application in hand, Laney left the shack at seven in the morning to get an early start. Today, she was not in a mood to bake, which was most unusual, especially since her display shelves were almost empty. But being the conscientious young woman that she was, soon the batter was prepared and in the oven baking. While waiting, Laney filled out the application, which, if accepted and approved, would allow Cassie to live with her. Cassie should have a room of her own, but how could she afford to add on a room? It was all she could do to keep her head above water with her current expenses. The business was growing daily, but when September arrived, the entire tourist population went home and daily receipts dwindled. Her plans had been to build an addition to the Sweet Shack with space for tables and chairs and a special place for holding cooking classes for children. Now, all of those plans must be placed on hold.

After the noon crowd left, Laney put a "Back in thirty minutes" sign in the window and went down the street to the Social Services office.

"Well, Laney, what brings you down here today?" trilled Mrs. Bryant, the local worker—as if she didn't know.

"I've come to apply for guardianship of Cassie."

"That's quite an undertaking for someone as young as you, Laney."

"Yes, but I have taken care of myself since I was twelve years old and gotten along just fine. In fact, I am a proud and successful business owner and plan to expand soon. Mrs. Bryant, this little girl has not had a mother since she was four. She suffered abuse in her foster home; Dr. Steve will testify as to her injuries. She experienced kidnapping and was traumatized so deeply that she was in a catatonic state until I told her she could live with me. If I need a character witness, Mr. Mac will vouch for me. Please don't be responsible for this child being disappointed and traumatized again."

"Laney you are aware that this must go before our board. I will be in touch."

"Thank you, Mrs. Bryant, I trust your judgment. I know you want the best for Cassie, too."

As Laney was leaving, Mrs. Bryant smiled and thought to herself, *This young girl will most likely be the best mother ever.* She picked up the phone and sent an email to all of the board members, calling for an emergency meeting the next evening.

Laney was edgy. She could think of nothing but Cassie and wondered if the board members would approve her as Cassie's guardian. What if they don't? What would she do? What would she tell Cassie? Now and then Speare/Daniel would sneak into her thoughts and crowd out Cassie, causing her to wonder how he really felt about Cassie living with her. Did it bother him? Would he want to be with her if Cassie were a permanent fixture? If he weren't coming back, then why waste time worrying ... and with that positive thought, she began to cry softly, saying, "Speare, I love you so much. I have loved you since I was twelve years old." Tears fell into her bowl of batter, making it a lost cause—good only for the garbage can. This was a first for Laney; she had never messed up batter before. She managed to get through the next forty-eight hours by planning the expansion of the Secret Shack. Finishing the last drawing, she was cleaning up all the paper she had used and scattered over the floor when the phone rang. Who could be calling at this hour?

"Laney, this is Mrs. Bryant with Social Services. I do hope I'm not calling too late."

"Not at all, Mrs. Bryant, I was working on the plans for the new addition."

"I've called to let you know that the board met, and I must admit, they were quite surprised that someone as young as you would want to take on such a mammoth responsibility."

"But Mrs. ..."

"Just listen Laney, let me finish."

"Sorry."

"Although they were concerned about your age, each member of the board agreed one hundred percent that of all people they know, you are the most responsible and loving and caring and will make a super guardian, even though you are so young."

"You mean I get to keep Cassie?"

"Yes, Laney. Congratulations. She is a precious child. After interviewing Cassie, also, we were convinced that you two belong together. Let me remind you, however, there is a six month probation period, and we will show up unannounced from time to time to check and see how the relationship is working."

"Oh, Mrs. Bryant, I am so happy and so very grateful. When can Cassie come?"

"Laney, you two are so alike, she asked the very same thing. How about tomorrow when you close the shop? I will bring her over with her belongings. She only has one suitcase."

"Thank you so much, Mrs. Bryant. I'll never let you down. I probably won't close my eyes tonight." As soon as she hung up, her only thoughts were of praise and gratitude. She knelt right where she was and thanked God for the trust placed in her. She added, "Please let me be the best mom Cassie can have."

Still finding it hard to believe, Laney was eager to call Mr. Mac, tell him the good news, and voice one of her concerns. "Mr. Mac, this has all happened so fast, I don't have an extra bed for Cassie and she won't have her own room. Do you have any suggestions?"

"As a matter of fact, I do. I have plans that I drew up when I thought Leanna and I would be living there, and another bedroom was the first room to be added."

"But I can't afford to add on, Mr. Mac."

"Laney, I saved the lumber and other material so that all one has to do is to add on. That would give me something to do in my spare time."

"But Mr. Mac, you're not hearing me. I don't have any extra money."

"Laney, on the contrary, you are not hearing me. I told you I think of you as a daughter, and since I am going to have a granddaughter, what would be more appropriate and give me more pleasure than to see the shack grow as intended with people living in it whom I love and who love each other? How happy that would make me!"

"Mr. Mac, you are the best. I can never repay you."

"Laney, believe me, dear girl, you already have."

Soon tears were trickling down Laney's cheeks again, but this time they were tears of joy.

CHAPTER 28

The trial was set for October, two months away, and life went on. The shack had a new room expressly for Cassie, the bakery was bursting at the seams, but Laney had not heard from Speare. Even Cassie would ask from time to time, "Are you sad, Laney?" Laney prayed that Speare had found his parents and that they had affirmed his identity. She prayed for his happiness and safety, and she prayed to have understanding.

Early one morning, there was a loud explosive sound near the front door, which actually shook the cottage. Both Cassie and Laney jumped out of their beds, terrified. They could see flames from the kitchen window rushing toward the shack. Laney dialed 911 immediately, and the fire truck arrived only minutes before the cabin would have been consumed by the fire. After they brought the fire under control, the firefighters discovered remnants of the material used to set the fire. One of the other firefighters walked around the shack looking for more evidence and spotted a bottle tied to a brick lying by the front door. He saw a note inside the bottle and asked Laney if she had seen it before. Laney reached for the bottle but the firefighter said, "No, you mustn't touch it; there may be fingerprints. I'll open it with gloves on and hold it to see if it says anything."

Laney read the note and felt the ground rise up to meet her as she blacked out. The shocked firefighter caught Laney just before she went all the way down. Another firefighter picked up the note and saw the threatening words — "NEXT TIME, CASSIE WILL BE OURS." The firefighter called 911 just as Laney was coming to. "I'm fine," whispered Laney. "Where is Cassie, somebody find Cassie." Laney was bordering on hysteria.

"It's okay, Laney, here's Cassie. She was hiding in the closet scared to death."

Cassie ran to Laney and threw her arms around her crying, "I was so scared, I thought something bad had happened to you."

"I'm okay, Cassie."

Mr. Mac had heard the news on his short wave radio and immediately informed the SBI. "We will send someone out right away to guard Cassie and Laney all night, and I will dispatch a couple of other men to start investigating this latest event. We definitely need to locate the chief and see what he is up to."

CHAPTER 29

In Richmond, things were not going as Speare had hoped. His call to Mr. Ward was rejected as a crank call. Speare was uncertain what to do next, so he walked into the neighborhood soda shop and found a seat over in the corner. Within seconds, an attractive young server approached Speare and said, "I'm Crystal, may I get you a drink?"

"An unsweetened iced tea will be fine."

"I'll bring it right out." Crystal returned with the tea and Speare casually asked if she knew the Wards who lived in the big house on the nearby hill. "There are no Wards, just Mr. Ward," she replied. "He and Mrs. Ward divorced about eight years ago. I understand they once had a son, but he disappeared ten years ago, also, and they have no clue where he is or what happened."

"How does one meet Mr. Ward?"

"That is very difficult. Mr. Ward thinks everyone is after his money. You see, a couple of young men have posed as his son recently, but he had their DNA checked and neither matched. About once a week, he'll visit us later in the day when most customers have gone. Some days he will strike up a conversation and other times he does not want to be disturbed. Today is Friday, so he may show up since he didn't come last week."

Sure enough, in about fifteen minutes, a distinguished looking man strolled into the shop. Crystal at once said, "Mr. Ward, would you like your usual seat?"

"That will be fine, Crystal, and I'll have a mocha frappuccino with a grilled pimento cheese sandwich." Mr. Ward sat adjacent to Speare. Speare could barely get his breath. He could be sitting within three feet of his father. He counted to twenty, holding his breath, to keep from hyperventilating. Speare must have looked distressed, because Mr. Ward said, "Son, are you okay? You looked as if you might pass out all of a sudden."

"I'll be okay. I received a shock and I'm not sure how to respond."

"Would you care to talk about it? Perhaps I could help you. My name is David Ward."

"I am called Speare, since I don't know my real name. A nurse at Duke Hospital gave me that name because I wrote so much while I was there. I was in a horrendous car accident on the Outer Banks in which two of my friends lost their lives. The doctor said I have amnesia. He thinks I'll get my memory back, but he doesn't know when. It has been five long years, and I had given up hope until lately when I have had several flashbacks. I lost my left leg and my right leg was badly mangled, requiring a year of surgeries and rehab. I'm sorry, I've never talked that much before, especially to a stranger. Please accept my apology."

This time Mr. Ward turned white.

"Sir, I didn't mean to freak you out. Are you all right, sir?"

"What do you do, Speare?"

"I work for the *Durham Daily News*. They were so kind to this unclaimed teenager; they offered me a part-time job during college with a full-time position right after I graduated. They were my adopted family."

"How old are you, Speare?"

"About twenty-four, I think. All of our identification had been removed by the time the Beach Patrol had arrived."

"Speare, come up to my house so we can continue our conversation; I may be able to help you."

"Thank you, sir, but I cannot impose on you."

"It will be my pleasure to talk to someone younger and with stories to tell. I may have a story to tell you as well."

"Very well, thank you, Mr. Ward." Speare and Mr. Ward walked up the hill to the big white house talking animatedly, enjoying each other's company. Speare was in awe upon entering this magnificent mansion. "What a lovely home," he exclaimed. "Did you grow up here?"

"Yes, my father built this house and my former wife and I, along with our young son, moved in after my parents passed away."

"Does your son still live with you?"

"Oh, no, and that is my story. Several years ago, we used to go as a family to the Outer Banks each summer and stay in my parents' cottage. My son loved the beach, but he became enamored with a young girl far beneath him socially who lived there year round. They were young but inseparable. My wife and I decided that if we moved away, that would end their relationship. True, we accomplished our goal, but our decision changed David's personality. At first, he stayed in his room and spent all of his time writing. Our relationship deteriorated until it became almost non-existent. David could not forget that we had arbitrarily separated him from a dear friend who understood him and who had endeared herself to him. At the time, we thought we were doing the right thing since he was so young. When he entered high school, his writings won the respect and admiration of his fellow classmates, and he was soon invited to join clubs and attend parties. His quick wit made people laugh, and at the same time, it hid the sadness that remained buried in David's heart. We learned that David dreaded coming home from school each day and never invited a friend for fear that his mother and I would engage in one of our fiery and loud arguments, usually brought on by her growing need for alcohol. I should have addressed that issue before it got out of control. After graduation, we heard that David and two of his friends had gone to the beach for a few days in his new convertible. He was just eighteen then with plans to enter Harvard in the fall. David was so smart that he had been offered scholarships to all the major colleges. In the meantime, we moved to the Dominican Republic and left word with our lawyer where we could be reached. Several weeks later, we received a call from him with the tragic news of an automobile accident. He told us that the *National News* carried a story of three unidentified young men who were in a terrible automobile accident on the Outer Banks. The story said that the car they were driving rounded the curve, straddling the centerline, and crashed into a power truck. Two of the young men did not survive the impact, and the driver was severely injured. The strange thing was that they were driving a nineteen eighty-nine Chevy and none of our boys had an older car. No identification was found on the passengers or in the car. The police assumed it was another case of stolen identity. We know that the third young man was badly injured and taken to a hospital, but we were never able to find out if this person was our David. My wife and I were experiencing a difficult time in our marriage that segued into a nasty and long-drawn out divorce, and finally two years later, a settlement. It was nasty! Because of the HPPA laws, no hospital would give out any information. I have not seen my son since. I hired detectives and enlisted the FBI's services, but neither were able to find out David's whereabouts."

"Mr. Ward, I'm so sorry for your loss. May I ask a personal question? Did your son have an identifying birthmark or anything that might distinguish him from someone else?"

"I had forgotten, but David had a strawberry mark above his right ear on his scalp. It was obvious when he was a baby, but as his hair began to thicken, you could no longer see the mark." Speare could not speak. He sat quietly until tears overflowed and ran down his cheeks. "Speare, what on earth is wrong? Did I say something to upset you?"

"No, Mr. Ward, but I might upset you with what I am going to show you." And Speare leaned his head toward Mr. Ward and parted his hair over his right ear to reveal a strawberry mark.

Mr. Ward gasped. "Oh, my God, can you be my David?"

"I don't know, Mr. Ward. It seems to add up, but we could have a DNA test so there would be no doubt, if you really want to know."

"Of course I want to know! My life has been so hollow since we lost David. My wife, your mother, became obsessed with being the social queen of the nation, and when her peers did not accept her, she started drinking until she was a full-blown alcoholic. Treatment did not help, and it became necessary to place her in an institution. About four years ago she died of cirrhosis of the liver and malnutrition."

"Oh, I'm so sorry. You have suffered much more than I have." David felt little sorrow since he had mourned the loss of his mother several years before.

"Speare, will you be willing to have a DNA test?"

"Yes, sir, the sooner, the better!"

CHAPTER 30

Laney was so concerned about Cassie's safety that she was almost paranoid, watching her nearly every second. Was the chief, who was out on bail, responsible for the threats? If only she knew what they were afraid she would tell. If only she could talk to her mother. Then Lacey remembered that Mr. Mac had alluded to her meeting her mom when she felt up to it. Laney called Mr. Mac and told him her wish. Mr. Mac said he would be back in touch. In one hour, Mr. Mac called back with disturbing news. He had found the apartment where Laney's mother was kept totally wrecked. Her mother was gone. It was obvious that a struggle had ensued. Someone was desperate to keep her silent. Mr. Mac was positive the chief was responsible for all of this, but he hid behind some of his henchmen. The chief wasn't that smart, but money talked. The story made the evening news along with the explosion and the fire directed at Laney and the threat against Cassie. Speare, now David, was watching the news with his newly found dad. The DNA test had positively identified that they were father and son, and a tearful but happy reunion followed. David heard the frightening news and without thinking, jumped up and said, "Oh, my dear God, Laney and Cassie are in danger. I must go and try to help them."

"David, please wait, I have a confession to make." And he told David exactly what had happened and asked if he ever could forgive him.

"Yes, Dad, I can and I will, but what are your feelings now? Because I care very much for this dear young woman and the child she is going to adopt, and this time, I will not let anyone come between us."

"David, your mom and I were so wrong. I only want you to be happy. I might even be able to help you with this problem. At least I could help protect Cassie so Laney would not be in constant fear."

"Dad, I cannot believe that we're together and you're willing to help me. I am so blessed. I can't wait for you to meet Laney and Cassie. You will learn to love them as much as I do. That will make me so happy."

The SBI received word that a small boat had left the marina at approximately three in the morning the same night Laney's mom had been abducted, and that a homeless man sleeping on the pier had seen a woman on the boat.

The Coast Guard was notified immediately and a network of Coast Guard boats was dispatched to the general area. It took only forty-five minutes for them to locate and apprehend the culprits and rescue Laney's mom. She was in a shocking condition, black and blue from having been beaten, and her left arm was most likely broken. She had suffered so much physical abuse through the years, but now she was ready to testify against this horrific man—the ringleader, the chief.

This time the bail was set so high that even the chief, with all of his illegal money, could not afford to meet it. His wife did a little secret dance of joy in her bedroom. She, too, was free at last from this madman who had fooled the public for so long. Laney's mom was taken at once to the hospital where her physical needs could be treated. Emotionally, it could take years for the horror she had suffered to be erased. Her daughter's safety had been her main concern and the sole motivation that had provided the needed strength to endure the atrocities inflicted by this monster, chief of the Beach Patrol. Her biggest regret was the many years she had been isolated from Laney and how she had succumbed to fear, allowing it to rule her every move. She could never make up all of that lost time with her precious daughter. It weighed heavily on her conscience.

CHAPTER 31

David, unaware that Laney thought he was not coming back, or at least not to her, was eager to return to the Outer Banks and introduce her to his dad. The miles passed so slowly. At last, he pulled up to the Sweet Shack and dashed inside, only to find Millie, the waitress who worked for Mr. Mac.

"Where is Laney," inquired David.

"She is at the hospital," responded Millie.

"What's wrong? Has something happened to Laney?"

"No, no. She is visiting someone in the hospital."

"You scared me. When will she be back?"

Looking at her watch, Millie replied, "In about an hour"

"Thanks, and will you let her know Speare's looking for her? I'll come back this afternoon."

Disappointed, to say the least, Speare returned to the car and said to his dad, "Let's go over to the Sea Wind and have a late lunch. I know you must be starving."

"That will be like old times."

David didn't respond for fear he might say something he would regret, such as, "You never had lunch with me," or "You had no idea where I was, nor did you care." However, he had found his father seemed to have changed, and he didn't want to break the spell. After they were seated, Mr. Mac came over, gave Speare a warm hug, and asked, "Does Laney know you're here?"

"No sir, Millie said she was at the hospital." Looking at his father and then back at Mr. Mac, who had been like a father to him as well, he said, "Mr. Mac, I would like for you to meet my father, David Ward. Turns out I am also David."

"What a pleasure this is," Mr. Mac said, shaking Mr. Ward's hand warmly. "Welcome, Mr. Ward! This calls for a celebration."

"Dad, this is the gentleman who has been such a big help to me. Perhaps we can celebrate tonight when Laney is free."

"We will definitely plan on that. Enjoy your lunch."

"Dad, I need to write a story of the latest developments of this case and send it to the paper before someone else gets the scoop. Then I want to go see Laney."

An hour later, David and his dad returned to the Sweet Shack. When they walked through the door, David spied Laney in the kitchen. He hurried toward her, saying, "I'm back, Laney."

Very formally, Laney answered, "It's nice to have you back, Speare. May I help you with something?"

"Laney, are you okay?"

"I'm fine, thanks. It's nice to see you again."

"Laney, it's me, Speare. I've found my dad and I want you to meet him."

"Oh, I didn't think you were planning to return, Speare. I was certain that once you were reunited with your dad, he would not want you to have anything to do with me."

A deep voice interrupted, "Laney, I'm David Ward, David's father, and I don't blame you for that. Please let me tell you how deeply sorry I am for how my wife and I behaved many years ago. Not trying to cast blame, but my wife, David's mother, was on her way to self-destruction. She was a sick woman. I should have been more firm. When we took David away and did not return the next summer, it was because she did not want David to get involved with you. She passed away four years ago, and I had almost become a recluse when David found me. We had so many years of catching up to do, and believe me, it has been wonderful. Please don't begrudge us that short time together." Turning to his son, he said, "David, I guess you took too much for granted. Obviously, Laney has no idea how you feel about her."

"Boy, am I dumb when it comes to women. Maybe you don't even care for me, Laney?"

"David, you mean more to me than life itself."

"Laney, I couldn't exist without you in my life. I love you so much."

"I've waited so long to hear those words, Daniel! I'm so happy you found your father and you two have reunited. But did you know that the adoption went through?" In response to his beaming face, she smiled back, then turned shyly to Mr. Ward. "Your dad might enjoy meeting her as well."

"I know he will. Where is she?"

"She's playing in the quad. I can see her from the front window. Here she comes now."

As Cassie got closer, she spied Speare and started running and yelling, "Speare, you came back. I knew you would." She jumped up and Speare caught her in a big bear hug, spinning her round and round.

"I missed you, Speare."

"I missed you, too, Cassie."

"Please don't leave again. Laney was so sad."

"Cassie, you are such a dear. Cassie, the reason I left was because I wanted to find my father, and I did. His name is Mr. David. My name is really David, too.

"Hi, Mr. Big David," she said, and everyone laughed.

"You are adorable, Cassie."

"Thanks, Mr. Big David, What is adorable?" Cassie asked innocently causing another burst of laughter.

"There is so much to talk about," Laney and Speare exclaimed simultaneously.

"Why don't we pick up supper at the Sea Wind and take it to the shack where we can eat and talk to our heart's content without being disturbed?"

"Mr. Ward, I hope you won't be uncomfortable, it isn't what you are used to. I live in what I call a shack at the other end of the island."

"Don't worry, Laney, I've learned so much these past ten years."

CHAPTER 32

The new trial was set to take place in two months, by which time Dr. Steve thought Laney's mom would be well enough to testify. In the meantime, the SBI was taking no chances. Agents guarded her room day and night. Undercover agents kept a close watch on Laney and Cassie, never letting them out of their sight. Cassie was so happy living with Laney. Her appetite flourished, and she even gained a few pounds, giving her a much healthier look. And Mr. Mac was building Cassie her very own bedroom. She was ecstatic.

The trial was getting closer; the security, tighter. You could feel the tension in the air. The townspeople talked animatedly about the latest news on the trial whenever they had conversation.

A new Beach Patrol chief replaced the crooked chief. People remained tuned to their local radio or TV station.

It was Saturday morning, only two days before the trial was to begin. Laney's mom, Mona, had been declared strong enough to testify. Suddenly, a special news alert interrupted the Friday morning cooking show.

"An attempt had been made on Mona O'Brien's life. There is evidence that someone impersonating a nurse gained access to NICU with the intent of murdering the key witness. The perpetrator managed to escape and, of course, an APB was sent out at once. Police are asking all citizens to stay inside. The suspect is armed and dangerous."

Mona had awakened with a start when a nurse pulled the covers back to give her an injection. When she recognized the nurse as the Beach Patrol imposter, she punched the button for a nurse and screamed at the same time. A nurse next door ran into the room and demanded to know what the man was doing.

"Move back or I'll kill both of you!" the man growled.

Another nurse, hearing the screaming and the threat, used her hospital phone to call hospital security and 911 before she dashed into the room. Once inside, she began talking calmly to the man. "I don't know who you are, but if you murder our patient, your sentence will be for a lifetime or worse, whereas if you don't do anything, most likely you will get off with a much lighter sentence. Think about it." She kept up this conversation until the SBI rushed into the room to grab the imposter.

Mona rolled over on her side away from the intruder to give the officers an opportunity to shoot this attempted murderer if necessary, but in a matter of seconds, he was in handcuffs and no longer a threat to Mona or anyone. At last, they had him—the chief's dirty boy, the one who had been responsible for all the incidents over the last several years. They were taking no chances this time; he was just as slippery as an eel and the only one who could rat on the chief. In fact, he knew just about everything bad the chief had ever done. Frisking this man revealed a pocket full of diamonds, approximately one million dollars' worth, which the chief had ordered him to place in several bank deposit boxes.

With the capture of the chief's right hand man, the trial was probably the shortest on record in spite of so many serious charges. The chief received a life sentence with no hope for parole. His sidekick received fifty years. It was a happy day for the citizens of the small coastal town. Everyone celebrated, and David's news story made national news on TV and the top papers in the country.

CHAPTER 33

A few months later, Laney, David, Cassie, and Mr. Big David enjoyed a leisurely supper with Cassie supplying them with a multitude of reasons to laugh. Aware that Laney and David had not seen each other for several weeks, Mr. Big David asked if it would be okay to take Cassie for a walk on the beach.

"Oh, may we, Laney?"

"I believe it will be just fine if you two think you can behave," joked Laney. And out they went …

David reached for Laney, and she went willingly into his arms. "Laney, I have missed you so much. You have become my life. Do you have any idea how important you are to me? Laney, I still cannot remember everything about my former life, but so much of it has returned. Can you love someone like that?"

"David, I have loved you forever, and I always will."

"Laney, would you consider marrying me and allowing me to adopt Cassie?"

"That is the most beautiful offer I have ever had. Yes, David, I would be honored to be Mrs. Daniel Speare David Ward."

When Mr. Big David and Cassie walked through the front door, David and Laney were grinning from ear to ear. "Guess what," they teased.

In unison, Cassie and Mr. Big David yelled out, "You're getting married."

Cassie was so excited and without hesitating, proclaimed for the world to hear. "David, you are going to be my daddy, and Mr. Big David, you will be my granddaddy, and Laney is already my mom. We will be the best family in the whole world."

Tears of joy flowed freely. As they hugged each other, their tears intermingled, washing over them and blessing them before flowing into the ocean that had brought them together.

From an ocean to a shack,

lives transformed there and back.

Sadness arrived, joy was proclaimed.

Love conquered all—love's sweet refrain.

EPILOGUE

The charming coastal town of Goose on the Outer Banks of North Carolina returned to normal everyday living. Thanks to the curiosity of a young reporter, Daniel Speare David Ward, the big crime ring that had been in the powerful clutches of the Beach Patrol chief for twelve years was obliterated by the SBI. It took almost a year to rehabilitate Mona, who had been a prisoner and abused for so long. Now, she was welcomed in Laney and David's home. David's father, David Sr., who loved his new role as grandfather, found himself enjoying Mona's company when she came to visit. Cassie was a happy little girl who made many friends. Two years after Laney and David were married down by the ocean's edge, a beautiful seven pound nine and a half ounce girl brought great pride and joy to this family. With sensitivity beyond her young years, Cassie loved taking care of her baby sister. Laney continued to look to Mr. Mac as a father to love and from whom to seek advice. Mr. Mac was definitely a member of this special family. The Sweet Shack was such a popular destination that it was enlarged in order to accommodate a room with tables so its patrons could sit and visit and enjoy the delectable goodies and coffee. Laney saw her wish come true with the opening of a baking school for young people. David was remembering more and more. His series on the coastal crime in Goose won a Pulitzer Prize for his paper. He retired from the paper to pursue his longtime dream to write novels. And once a week, the Wards would descend on the popular Sea Wind Restaurant, where Mr. Mac, Mona, and Mr. David Sr. would join them for a fun-filled meal, but only after offering their heartfelt thanks to the Father they knew and trusted and loved.

QUESTIONS TO PONDER

1. What is your opinion of a thirteen-year-old girl living alone?
2. Were David's parents right or wrong to take David away in order to sever his relationship with Laney? Was it concern for David, or did another reason motivate this action? What other way might this situation been handled?
3. Do you believe Laney's feelings for David kept her from dating others? If so, why did she consent to go out with Speare?
4. Do you believe David's parents exhausted all efforts to find David? Did their shortcomings/problems prohibit a more ongoing search?
5. Should the townspeople have been more aggressive and elected a new Beach Patrol chief, or were they unsure of the extent of his wrongdoing?
6. Did you approve of Mr. Mac's relationship with Laney? What kind of love did he have for this young girl?
7. Laney was mature for her age, but did she have the parenting skills necessary to raise a child? Was Laney too young to adopt Cassie? If so, why, and if not, why not?
8. Was David a good role model for an amputee? Did he use his handicap unselfishly?

9. Was there anyone in David's life who was influential in teaching him about faith and trust and loving others unconditionally? Was he affected by this teaching?
10. The shack played a significant role in the lives of the wealthy young man and the poor young lady. Was it more than just a dilapidated old building that provided shelter? Explain.
11. Should David have called Laney while with his father? What do you think kept him from contacting Laney?
12. Should David have forgiven his father? What are we taught?
13. Who in this story ministered, through their work, by their actions, and their words?
14. What did you learn from this story? Were you able to relate to any of these relationships?

Printed in the United States
By Bookmasters